HITTAZ 6

Chapter AK Verse 47

LOU GARDEN PRICE, SR.

URBAN AINT DEAD

James T Vaughn Correctional Center, Smyrna DELAWARE

For tablet connection. Download the gettingout.com app.

Contact Publisher at www.urbanaintdead.com

Email: urbanaintdead@gmail.com

Print ISBN: 979-8-9908882-2-7

SOUNDTRACKS

Scan the QR Code below to listen to the Soundtracks/Singles of some of your favorite U.A.D titles:

Don't have Spotify or Apple Music?
No Sweat!
Visit your choice streaming platform and search URBAN AINT DEAD.

Currently on lock serving a bid?
JPay, iHeartRadio, WHATEVER!
We got you covered.
Simply log into your facility's kiosk or tablet, go to music and search
URBAN AINT DEAD.

UAD Presents

Like & Follow us on social media:

FB - URBAN AINT DEAD

IG: @urbanaintdead

Tik Tok - @urbanaintdead

Submission Guidelines

Submit the first three chapters of your completed manuscript to urbanaintdead@gmail.com, subject line: Your book's title. The manuscript must be in a .doc file and sent as an attachment. The document should be in Times New Roman, double-spaced, and in size 12 font. Also, provide your synopsis and full contact information. If sending multiple submissions, they must each be in a separate email. Have a story but no way to submit it electronically? You can still submit to URBAN AINT DEAD. Send in the first three chapters, written or typed, of your completed manuscript to:

URBAN AINT DEAD
P.O Box 448
Maybrook, NY 12543

DO NOT send original manuscript. Must be a duplicate.
Provide your synopsis and a cover letter containing your full contact information.
Thanks for considering URBAN AINT DEAD.

To all those who are becoming a part of my IGWB, LLC company: Chad Prissy, Kelly Cobb (Dover DE), my homie Petey Clark, and everyone else (Honey B). IGHOSTWRITEBOOKS523@gmail.com. Thanks.

He's a man. A man's man. In the corrupted machismo of Cosa Nostra, that was the highest accolade, incorporating notions of loyalty to friends; strength of heart, mind, and body; charisma; leadership; and most of all, criminal daring and know-how.
-Jerry Capeci

Part One

"BACK TO THEM BROOKLYN STREETS"

"1, 2, 3, 4, 5, 6, 7, 8, 9 / It's The Ten Crack Commandments, what!? Niggas can't tell me nuttin' bout this coke / can't tell me nuttin' about this crack, this weed / my husslin' niggas / niggas on the corner, I ain't forget you niggas / my Triple Beam niggas!!!"

-From: The Greatest of All-Time Notorious B.I.G.

CHAPTER 1

The Braga Safehouse
<u>Chicago, ILL</u>

JOKER DIDN'T WASTE another moment in retrieving Yolie Santana's rotting corpse from Don Braga's Chicago safehouse where Bibleman had left it stashed at. However, a body wasn't something one could just toss out with the day's ordinary refuse. If the ravens had detected even one small scintilla of it they'd be swarming it likes bees around a honeycomb - picking the rancid meat off the bones. And all it would take was one nosey neighbor for it to be discovered by police.

That's the last thing Joker wanted. He had a desire, a duty, to keep EIE members clean. They may have a deal going with the government but that didn't mean they had a free pass to commit wholesale homicide. And, God forbid, if other EIE members found out about what Bibleman Reed had done. He had a high position in the organization, not just as Joker Red's right hand, but he was EIE's "spiritual leader." He was like Martin Luther King, Jr. to them in a way.

"Gotdamn you, Yolie," Joker whispered to himself when he had learned of it. "What the *fuck?*!"

Joker felt somewhat responsible in that moment. She had taken

3

Joker's advice about her pregnancy to Bible: to inform him that there was a possibility that he was not the father of her baby. Joker had felt that Bible would understand and even embrace it as his own upon its birth. He couldn't have ever been more wrong.

"I snapped, boss," Bible admitted to Joker a few days prior. "She told me-"

"I *know* what she told you," Joker had cut him off as they had placed her body into the bathtub at the safehouse apartment. "And *you* – zero talkin' about any of it. I ain't the judge of your journey. From this point you go lay low in the vehicle. Sleep or somethin'. I'll take care of disposal."

Bible went on out to the GMC Yukon Denali, hopped in, and closed the driver's side door. He turned the stereo system on and set the iTunes Music on auto-play. *Blues*. As Muddy Waters belted out the class hit, "*40 Days, 40 Nights,*" he realized why Joker didn't want him inside of the apartment while he disposed of Yolie's remains. Joker worried about the emotional toll it would have on Bible because it would get ugly…nauseating…sad…

First, Joker had to use an electric wood saw to cut her head off. Then he used a sturdy, handheld garden shear to slice her up into even smaller pieces. Her arms were cut down into six parts. A sledge-hammer easily crushed her bones to make the process smoother. Then her legs were split into ten sections.

He heated the cooking oil and prepared a fried chicken batter inside a large black plastic trash bag. He threw every seasoning he could find into the flour, pancake mix, and baking powder: salt, pepper, curry, garlic, lemon pepper, Cheyenne, jerk chicken seasoning, and others. He tossed smaller body sections inside the mix and shook it up like a chef competing on Fox Television's *"HELL'S KITCHEN."* He dropped half of her body inside a turkey deep fryer. And, minutes later, the other half was dropped inside a second deep fryer.

While those halves were frying he cut out her entire jaw. He used a screwdriver to knock all of her teeth out. He simply flushed her teeth and fingertips down the toilet along with other small pieces of her. He checked the deep fryers. Once the meat was done he stored it inside of a large clear plastic storage tub. There was one (tub) that held meat and another that held her bones. He packed both tubs away into extra-large laundry bags that were made out of nylon material. One was red and the other white.

He was a sophisticated criminal with a mind that was supremely aware of DNA fiber evidence, and what police crime scene experts looked for. So, when he cleaned up the blood he knew that he had to trick even the police's "Luminol" test which criminals always forgot about. He cleaned from top to bottom and then he cleaned again.

He stripped, bagged up everything he'd been wearing, and showered. He got dressed in black jeans, a beater, a black T-shirt, which had a magnificent sketch of Kobe Bryant on the front and Gianna Bryant on the back, butter Timberland classics, dark wrap-around Ray Bans with a fitted black baseball cap with the iconic letters "BLM" emblazoned across the front, ("Black Lives Matter"). He sent Bible a text to come on back up. Minutes later Bible was at the door. Joker handed him the two laundry bags. "Don't matter how you carry 'em. They're sealed tight," Joker told him.

Bible nodded and walked down the stairs with Joker behind him. They got out to the Denali and opened up the rear cargo hatch. They loaded it up and Joker instructed Bible to drive them through Chicago's mean streets.

It had taken Joker several hours to get the tough part over with. Now all they had to do was discard the meat and bones…

When the black luxury SUV drove through West Garfield Park they noticed that there was a massive police presence on 67th Street and Morris Avenue where the neighborhood liquor store and bodega was. As it turned out, one more unarmed black man had been beaten and killed at a traffic stop. The Black man - 54-year-old Donald Clark - was or could later be seen on a bystander's cellphone video arguing with two white officers over a "failure to signal" violation when one of the officers decided to arrest him for a bogus disorderly conduct duct charge. The officer tried to slam his head against the car and ended up shooting him and claiming that the decedent had reached for a weapon. In the video, however, the black man's hands could be seen at all times.

He'd never tried to reach anywhere for anything except for when he had defiantly said, *"Arrest me!? Arrest me?!? Whatever den, you stupid stinkin' racist pig motherfucker! Let's go den, ya bitch!"*

And right when he had said that his hands, both hands, were in a motion thrusting themselves behind him. That's when he was shot in the chest - *twice*. That particular incident had happened in Burnside but once the video hit Facebook, the entire country was pissed off. The cops thought that they had gotten away with it because it happened at 2:00 AM.

There had been two days of marching and rioting and picket signs. *The usual "Peaceful Protests" that racist people in power laugh at and have no worries about. No one cared. White cops were promoted for shooting "niggers." They could go out tomorrow and kill Spike Lee, Byron Allen, Dave Chapelle, Evergreen, Ava Duvernay, and Leslie Jones... and all peoples gon' do is much and sing that 'We Shall Overcome' bullshit. Fuck that!* His name was Isaiah O'Neal but he was better known throughout West Garfield Park, Chatham, South Shore, Riverdale, and other sections of the Chi as "Poke-A-Dot" - for his feared reputation with a gun and an ice pick.

Those were his thoughts, his words, his way of thinking. He was a well-respected hitta in the streets, a gun for hire with nothing to lose. He'd lost his mother to a heart attack the year before after COVID-19 had gotten her. His father was serving triple life in the feds. And he was only thirty-three years old. No wife. No children. He was recently diagnosed with pancreatic cancer. He had always despised cops but as a matter of respect for the streets, he'd let them live. And, even with the reputation he'd carried for 17-18 years on the streets, the cops had stayed in their lane.

If the police had ever tried him he would've had all their little cop buddies out there carrying that casket and blowing on them fucking bagpipes. But, lucky for them, it never had to go down that way.

Well at least not until today.

Joker and Bible had not heard all the details yet but Poke-A-Dot had ambushed Chicago Police Officers Luke Bundy and Nicholas Ackerman at Winchell's Donuts earlier in the day. Both officers had been placed on administrative desk duty pending the outcome of the investigation of the shooting death of Donald Clark. Poke-A-Dot already knew how the *'investigation'* would turn out, he was currently broadcasting online. *These stinkin' peckerwoods will get off scot-fuckin-free. Anybody - white, black, whatever - who think that Floyd's trial changed anything is a goddamned fool... That George Floyd shit was these whities throwin' you dumb niggas a bone to shut ya mouths up! The DEA and Border agents work with the Mexican drug cartels. Once or twice a year they show the world a couple hundred pounds of coke for the same reason! To stick a bone in Congress' and the fuckin President's mouths to sign that Crime Bill budget check!*

Joker would see all of this online later but this man - Isaiah "Poke-A-Dot" O'Neal - was going on a nonstop rant about Chicago's dirty cops and why he had shot and killed the two who had killed the unarmed motorist, Donald Clark, in Burnside. Poke-A-Dot had killed Luke Bundy. Nick Ackerman had pulled through but was in critical condition. Poke-A-Dot had grabbed four children as hostages from inside his apartment building when he saw the cops roll up six cars deep. With the cops being shot, one dead of the two, and now the situation was even more grim with four children being held at gunpoint. That's why there were so many police present, including S.W.A.T.

"Turn up the alley off 63rd Street," Joker directed Bible. "Stop at green gates."

Bible drove up the alley, went four houses up, and parked along a small inlet where the green gates were. He knew Joker was about to feed the "Hell Dogs," as they were nicknamed. Inside the smelliest backyard in the neighborhood were three enormous Doberman Pinschers. They were extremely mean dogs that were kept in the yard and never seen out walking with their owner(s) on a leash.

Anytime neighborhood children walked up the alley they would run as fast as they could because the very sound of those Hell Dogs barking struck fear inside of them. It was so funny to see how frightened the kids were of these dogs and even funnier because of how goofy they looked running past their yard.

"Looks like every cop in the city is up 67 but watch the mouth of the alley anyway," Joker told Bible. "I'm 'bout to feed 'em."

"What about the other end of the alley?"

"It's a '*Dead End*' alley," Joker reminded him, irritated.

"Bible forgot."

Joker removed the plastic container with the fried remains in it and took it over to the tall green wooden fence. He lifted the top off of it and threw the entire thing over the fence. The dog started scarfing down the fried human meat. They fought with each other a little, but there was plenty of Yolie's meat to go around. They didn't want to bark at Joker that much after that.

He returned to the back of the Denali and grabbed the container with the bones inside of it. He also retrieved the sledgehammer and using one hand, began to smash the dry bones while they were inside of the box-shaped container. The skull was already sliced up into several pieces. It didn't take long to smash up at all. Then he emptied it on the ground and smashed it even more until the bones were crushed to gravel-like pieces and dust. He put it all back into the container and opened up a can of paint. He poured the paint down into the container and threw the container into a nearby trash dumpster.

"C'mon!" Joker called over to Bible. "We done wit it."

Bible drove them out of West Garfield Park, and they headed back across town to Don Braga's safehouse.

"I wanna see how it smells," Joker said as he entered the apartment. Joker walked around. "That's cool… a relief cause I thought the Pine-Sol and bleach was too loud."

"It's only loud while wet," Bible told him.

Joker nodded and went to shower once more after breaking a sweat dealing with the Hell Dogs and the bones. They were only there for nearly an hour before taking the Denali in for full detail and arranging for it to be picked up by Vinnie for safekeeping.

Before leaving Chicago via private jet, they went to Stark's Steakhouse. They had three maybe even four hours to burn before their plane would be ready, frustrating Joker.

"It's *our* pilot," Joker complained to Bible. "Ask Jesus to make the pilot come to work earlier."

Bible shook his head. "The last thing Bible do is play with the Lord on frivolous matters. We have to thank the Lord that the pilot is late. Or else if we ask the Lord for a thing and that thing is granted …Ever hear the saying: Be careful what you ask for? Well, we *especially* gotta be careful when asking *God* for it!"

"This whole trip has sapped my energy," Joker sighed as he looked around the restaurant. "It's packed in this bitch."

"The steaks are perfect," Bible reminded him. "Bible hungry."

Joker stood up and walked off. But he came right back and picked up his phone. "It's loud in here and Boss Lady's callin'."

"Who, Leah?" Bible joked.

Joker smiled. "The other Boss Lady, Madam Butterfly. Yo, nigga, I'm steppin' outside for a coupla phone calls. Order me *twenty-four-inch* tenderloins, *twenty* T-bones, and at least fifteen pounds of that spicy sweet Spanish rice they got. Tell 'em it don't haveta be packed separate but it-"

"You gotta tell 'em all that," Bible waved him off. "I'll send her to you outside if she wants a big tip."

Joker gave him a stack of cash and put in his take-home bulk order before exiting to make some telephone calls.

CHAPTER 2

Stark's Steakhouse
<u>Chicago, ILL</u>

JOKER PAID the limousine driver outside of Stark's and instructed him to stay put while he and Bible had dinner and dessert inside. Joker finished up on the telephone and went back to their table.

Their waitress was a black girl named Roxanna. She was darker than a chocolate chip, plain looking, a long weave of black and blonde hair, 5'4" tall. and a beautiful wedding band and engagement ring set on her left ring finger.

"Your take-home order is still being boxed and sealed," she updated Joker as she laid out their dinners for them.

"You can bring the dessert out, too, Roxanna," Joker told her, glancing at his phone.

Bible was grinning all through dinner. Joker idly wondered what he kept smiling or laughing about. But Joker was busy texting back and forth with his wives while eating the delicious steak.

"Youse about a smiley ass mufu-" Joker finally looked over his right shoulder and that's when he saw *her*.

No. Scratch that.

That's when he saw *them*. They were unbelievably pretty. They were so hot that Joker had to look twice. One of them looked like she could be white or even pass for Latina. She had amazing silvery eyes that looked like something seen out of one of those Victoria's Secret Valentine's Day shows. She was dressed in a revealing top and shorts that showed off lovely thighs and legs. Joker's eyes dropped to the floor and noticed the black designer Dior sandals that showcased "foot model" - beautiful feet with several small red and gold floral tattoos on them.

"You met her before?" Joker asked Bible. "You doin' all this smilin' and flirting wit them."

"Bible flirt?" the enormous man asked, pointing at himself. "Girls flirt. She flirts at Bibleman."

"*Girl* a goddess," Joker told him.

"She not want Bible." He put his head down. "Bible unlovable. Look at me…like Yolie."

Joker dropped his fork. *Damn.* "Ayo, you need to boss up, homie. Even I get turned down. You just need-."

"You have a house full of pretty girls," Bible reminded him.

"Even the ugliest dog in da kennel gotta get lucky one day," Joker told him. "Plus, you know how I inherited them."

The white/Latina girl was with a lovely, brown-skinned, black girl. They stood up to leave and as they walked past, the white chick stopped next to Bible with a big grin on her face.

"Hi!" she said all bubbly, "I'm Charlotte Anders. Can I grab your bicep?"

Joker stared right at the "V" between the legs of the black girl because it was encased in tight white *Fabletics* that a lot of women were wearing nowadays to jog or run around in.

Bible stood up, a little surprised. "Me? Bible's bicep?"

She nodded. "Um hm. What's your name?"

Bible made a muscle and smiled as her little hands encircled his tree trunk like muscles and squeezed. She saw the way his body was rippling beneath his wife-beater.

"Bible Reed," he told her. "Eustace Bible Reed. That's Joker Red."

"Girl, he's *Mr. Universe*! And super tall…rock solid!" The white/Latina babe told her girlfriend.

"I'm Ciarán Hazlett," the black girl introduced.

"She drunk?" Joker whispered, prying his eyes away from her pussy print.

Ciarán giggled. "No! Ha! Ha! Ha!" she laughed harder. "She just outgoing."

"You got a wife or girlfriend, dontcha?" Charlotte asked Bible as she held her pelvic area.

"Well, I did have Yol-"

"Bible, answer direct, bro," Joker elbowed him.

"No. Bible don't have anyone," he stated somberly. "Your stomach hurts?"

"No, I drank a lot of water," she replied. "We'll be right back, Hercules."

"He's not Hercules," Ciarán stated as they walked away. "He *Black Thor*."

The white/Latina girl was the taller of the two. The shorts she had on were made of thin gray flimsy material with pink lines along the sides and she was nude underneath. She dropped as few coins on the floor when she was about a few strides away from Bible. As Charlotte bent over at the waist to pick them up Joker and Bible could see the paper-thin silky material riding north in the deep groove of her ass crack like it was climbing up into the contours of her closely guarded secrets. Bible turned around so he wouldn't be caught stalking her baby fist-shaped pussy. Joker must've been thinking the same thing because they both turned away at the very same second!

When the girls disappeared around the corner out of sight from them, they burst out laughing. "Char! Did you drop that money on purpose?" Ciarán asked.

"No, I'd die!" Charlotte whispered. "Why, did my Black Thor look in there?"

"They both was lookin', girl!" Ciarán revealed.

Charlotte wanted to scream. "Bitch, and I don't have no panties on! I'm so embarrassed right now."

Ciarán gasped. "Why not?!"

"I was on my period!" Charlotte cried, making an angry face. "She ain't have no air all week. God! I can't go back out there. He'll think I'm a whore!"

Back out at the table, Bible was saying to Joker, "Son, Bible says on all he cares for… I could see the impressed of her anus!"

"You mean the *impression*?"

"Yeah, that."

"The imprint," Joker stated. "She got a *pretty* pussy."

"On all Bible care for!" he repeated. "I mean, if I ever get her mad and she tell me to kiss her ass, Imma kiss her entire A-S-S-H-O-L-E. Right on that impression imprint."

Joker was cracking up at the way Bible spoke and put words together. He knew that Bible had taken fire in the wars, and it had affected his speech some, so he was only laughing along *with* him not *at* him. But the way he spoke was hilarious.

"Ciarán bad as fuck, too," Joker was saying. "But that white girl all over you. I think I saw the crinkle winkle, too. Her shit looks like one of them tiny things that go on the bolt. You know the nuts and bolts?"

Bible laughed. "Nah, her shit looks like the fuckin *Star of David*! Jew booty! Ha! Ha! Ha!"

More laughter.

"She got a small ass pussy," Joker mentioned. "But that shit's deceivin'."

"I saw that," Bible stated.

"How many bitches did you fuck when you got away from Bellevue Wing?" Joker asked.

"You mean the VA Hospital, nigga?"

"It was a joke, fool," Joker told him. "Bellevue is the infamous psych ward in New York."

Bible saw the humor. "Oh. I was in the psych ward. First off, the V.A. got psychiatric help. No psyche ward. I heard of Bellevue Hospital in Manhattan. I almost got Baker Act'd once and sent there but the cops that picked me up were Marine niggas. They took me to the V.A. up Harlem that night."

Joker tilted his head to the right. The women were returning.

"Where in New York City y'all from?" Ciarán asked as they came back.

"It's all in y'all's accents."

"Brooklyn," Joker disclosed.

While the women had been in the bathroom they had gotten themselves "freshened up" and changed. Charlotte had put on some fashion-forward white satin Chanel shorts, pink thongs, and a matching Chanel hoody and she had thrown her long dark hair high up on top of her small girly head in a comfortable bun. Her left leg was nearly bare whereas her right leg was fully adorned with professionally crafted tattoos of doves, a visibly pregnant nude woman in a sexually explicit missionary position, and something else Bible was unable to make out.

"Y'all wanna sit with us for dessert?" Bible invited them.

Ciarán noticed the wedding band on Joker's left ring finger. "Are both of y'all married?"

Joker shook his head. "Just me."

Joker could read the dismay in Ciarán's chemistry. "Don't worry 'bout nothin' though, shorty."

"Hmph," she uttered. "I'm five feet seven so I'm not that short, Mister Joker Red."

"How tall are you, pretty white girl?" Bible asked Charlotte.

She punched Bible's right arm. "Ow! You are a brick wall, man!" She hurt her knuckles hitting him.

Bible smiled.

"I'm Cuban American," she stated. "That means I'm black."

"Oh, I am sorry, apologize, apologetic," Bible nearly stuttered. "Tell Bible about Miss Charlotte Anders. Tell Bible and Bible remember."

Charlotte and Ciarán looked at Bible a little bit strangely at first, but Charlotte waved it off.

"Hold up, ladies," Joker looked at his watch. "We are killin' about two and a half more hours, cause we headin' to Florida tonight."

Ciarán frowned. "That's unfortunate because we're from Kingsland, Georgia. Our rental car is all packed up so we can start the drive since the traffic jam died."

"That's our direction," Joker announced. "Y'all fly?"

"Yeah but y'all goin' to Florida," Charlotte pointed out. "We leave the rental at the airport so we're stuck in Florida. Where in Florida?"

"West Palm Beach," Joker said.

"We were visiting my grandma in Cicero," Charlotte said, pulling out her billfold from her purse. She removed $360. "We can get another rental down there. We use your card and we'll cover it with-."

"That's ridiculous," Joker said, shaking his head. "I meant – the plane is ours."

The women looked at each other.

"Oh!" Charlotte laughed. "Serious?"

Bible found a photo of the airplane on his cellphone. "EIE, Inc. We have *airplanes*. Plural."

"Oh, ooouu!" Ciarán swooned. "My goodness, y'all own it. What…mm."

"It's a real frickin' G6," Charlotte guessed. "I'll see what she did. Mm. Mum. Mama teaches that early. Mum's the word!"

They had dessert first. Bananas Foster and vanilla ice cream made at the restaurant.

"We grew up in Brooklyn around the same way but it wasn't until we were in basic training together that we became brothers," Joker explained to the two attentive women. "Bibleman took an incendiary fragment to the head that was meant for me because I was the sergeant of my squad. He seen that fire comin' because incendiary projectiles are on fire, and they glow at night. The enemy shot hundreds of them at our position. I was exposed. The rest of my unit was clinging to safety behind two rocks on the mountainside when a fresh barrage of enemy fire came. Bibleman Reed knew he'd be hit but I swear on everything, I make sure the men and women in my unit are safe before I run for safety. And this mufucka left safety to take one for me. Show 'em, B."

Bibleman showed them the long scar on the back of his head and neck. He turned all the way around in his seat and rubbed along the old scar with his fingers…from the top of his head – the scalp area - to where the brain stem and base of the skull met.

"Here to here was splattered open," Joker continued. "Fortunately, the incendiary projectile fragmented first because if one small fragment can do this much damage imagine if the entire thing exploded inside his brain. The other flip side – irony – is that he was fortunate that the fragged piece was on fire when it hit 'im because it cauterizes the wound."

"Caut – a what?" Charlotte asked. "You mean *burnt* it?" her voice was choking.

"Yeah, cauterize…to burn or sear with a cautery," he explained. "So, he wouldn't bleed out up on that mountain."

"Wow, so…" Charlotte's skin was all red now, her emotions were raw and she started to cry. "His brain was damaged durin' that fight?"

Joker had to dry his own eyes. "He saved my life," Joker admitted soulfully. "And I love his ass for that."

"Bibleman, I'm not emotional right now cause I'm sad," she said, gasping and trying to control her tears. "I'm so happy. This is such a sweet story of friendship, brotherhood, and American glory. You military guys are *something*."

"Char," Ciarán said. "We met some bonafide soldiers tonight."

Joker looked at his phone. "The pilots texted us that we got sixty minutes. Where's y'all's car?"

"In the parking lot," Ciarán said. "Don't mess up y'all flight schedule. We'll fly into Florida with y'all and drive back up. Kingsland is in Camden County. We're right next to Jacksonville so."

"Look," Joker waved her off. "I got a helicopter down there; I'll send you back on the jet. Don't worry about nothin'. Come on, B."

Joker pulled out a clip of cash and walked around the restaurant with Bible handing out $20's, $50's, and $100's to everybody. Outside, they gave Ciarán and Charlotte $1000 each. There was awesome power in impressing new females.

"Y'all don't need to do that," Charlotte said after they put their luggage into the trunk of the waiting Mercedes-Benz limousine. "We have jobs to return to in Kingsland."

Bibleman and Joker merely waved them off.

CHAPTER 3

"I live a polyamorous life"
<u>Casablanca Hotel, Miami</u>

THEY ALL FELL asleep on the jet. Before they knew it they were landing at Miami International Airport at 4:00 AM. Joker had a Mercedes Sprinter take them to the Casablanca Hotel where he checked them into one of their rooftop apartment suites. Each apartment had multiple rooms, a swimming pool on the roof, a fully-stocked kitchen and bar, Jacuzzi, and several bathrooms.

The first thing Joker did was take a shower and make himself comfortable in one of the rooms. He was tired so he stripped down to his boxers and laid out on the bed. He called Ciarán into the room with him.

"You got a robe on," he observed.

She grinned, "I just showered and lotioned my body when you called me."

"Whatchu' 'bout to do?" he inquired.

"Nothin'. Leave them two lovebirds alone." Ciarán stated, referring to Bible and Charlotte. "They want each other."

"I'm happy y'all ain't see the money and the life we lived first," he said. "That shit just happened organically."

Ciarán nodded. "Y'all are rich and it never showed until y'all said you owned a plane."

"C'mere. Lemme talk to you," Joker said as he laid back on the bed with his back against the pillows. "Lemme smell how nice you smell."

She smiled.

She sat up on the bed, near where he was.

"I live a polygamous life," he started. "When my polyamory started I had thirteen women. The number one, my Queen Wife, Uzenna, is my legal wife in the American law's eyes. I had rescued them, or was the mastermind and army general, who freed them from the grip of mobsters."

"Thirteen women," Ciarán said. "Being sex trafficked?"

He nodded. "Them chicks all knew each other since diapers and elementary school down south. So they were all tight. The other twelve women wanted more security. A family unit. *Let's all have a baby by him and they'll be brothers and sisters.* But meanwhile, my babies all wanted their named changed to my last name."

Ciarán stared a hole into his face. "And none of this was your idea? The thirteen babies, the same name…?" her questions trailed off.

"Listen…" Joker held up a right hand. "On God. I'd love to take all the credit but these babes turned out to be the craftiest, most intelligent people I ever met. So all thirteen get pregnant and have their names changed. I love all of 'em."

"Seriously," Ciarán said, doubting him. "Cause a man can love pussy as -"

Joker shook his head emphatically. "How many people you grow up wit? In the same household?" he shot back, setting up the point he was making.

"Nine," she admitted.

"How many cousins and other family y'all got around the U.S.?" he continued. "Including nieces, nephews, aunts, uncles, in-laws…?"

"Fifty, sixty, I don't know," she said. "A lot."

He nodded. "My point is that you *love* those you live with and give your every day to, right? I mean compared to the 50 family members you got scattered around."

"That's kinda different but I ain't screwin' none of 'em," she said.

"You know what I mean. It ain't all just fuckin'," he explained. "I came outta prison over five years ago with like fifteen hundred in my pocket and now I run an empire that knocks down seventy-five million a month. Dick alone can't build that."

"Okay. You got me there," she said. "I see the point."

He sighed. "But enemies came one day and set off bombs meant to take me out. Instead, they wiped out four of my wives and four of my children. Then I lost one more wife. So, I have eight wives in total. Thirteen toddlers."

She shook her head, having to take a breather.

"Why are you tellin' me this?" she asked him.

"Charlotte and my best friend clicked and I felt I *had to* open the door on my life for you," he informed her in a sincere tone. "I coulda just went on to West Palm Beach without schoolin' y'all first."

"Is that why we in Miami?" Ciarán said in a sultry tone as she shed the robe she wore.

She had on a yellow G-string bikini by Prada and she smelled like cocoa butter and vanilla lotion. Her skin glowed. His feet were soft and pretty. She sat Indian style, facing him with a shy smile. Joker's dick got harder than deciphering the Latin language.

"Yeah, so we could get to know each other better," he said, pulling her over so that she straddled his lap. "You should know what you about to get yo'self into, right?"

Her sweet G-string-covered cunt was bald and leaking her feminine creams all between her thighs. It took very little time to get her wet and dripping. She didn't tell Joker but while she'd been in the shower, she had masturbated to thoughts of him fucking her and sucking her breasts. Nothing got her off more than a breast man who loved 32D-sized breasts – which was her size.

"You mean know each other like this?" She could feel his golf-ball-like dickhead balloon even harder inside of his boxers as that huge anaconda laid up towards his belly button. She gyrated her dripping clitoris in 360-degree circles – in up and down humping gestures. She looked at his pulsating organ and was surprised to see that it was so elongated and thick that it had thrust up out of the elastic waistband of his Marc Jacob boxer underwear. "This. What. You. Wanna. Get. To. Know?"

"Shit. You should stop, Ciarán," he whispered as he felt her pull his boxers off. He lifted his ass to help her. "I just don't think…" All the while his penis grew harder.

"*Please*, Joker? It's been almost six months since I had some," she was nearly begging him but her hands were shaking as she stroked his hairless scrotum. It was as big as a juicy grapefruit. No. Big didn't describe what she was seeing; *humongous* was more like it. And *heavy*. "My fuckin' God!" she gasped.

She squeezed, pulled, and massaged the unusually large sack and stared with amazement in her pretty brown eyes as his pre-cream squirted out of the giant corona. "Oooooouuuuueee, look! It's bubbling out! Joker, I can't fit that thing in me. It's massive! How big is it?"

"A foot," he answered her.

"It's a porno movie dick," she mentioned as she re-straddled him. "And my pussy is so small, but, mm!"

Slowly and calculatedly, she rocked those shapely hips. As he placed sexy love bites on her hard nipples, sucking them left to right, she rubbed her pussy firmly against the enormous dickhead. It turned her on even more as he controlled her hips, making her rake her cunt a complete foot down and up the hot and hard length of his penis. Her leaking cunt drew wet him all over, soaking him. The flimsy material of the G-string stretched so much that she was able to work a portion of his length up inside of that juicy pink hole.

She thought he'd split her little pussy and make it bleed so she froze and took a deep breath.

CHAPTER 4

Meth Man Ace
Jasper, Florida

JASPER, Florida, was a rural town that lay on the northern border and was dotted with landowners who farmed fruits such as oranges, lemons, strawberries, and peaches. Others farmed much more in-demand commodities needed to fill the local stores and farmers markets such as onions, tomatoes, lettuce, corn, beef, pork, and dairy products.

But what caught Meth Man Ace's eye as he hired dozens of contractors to come in and help develop his land was not the ordinary property owners – the rich elite in the area – but the so-called "poor white trash" who lived in the county. Ace had a sense that the rich elite may have had all the money in the town but not the power.

"I think you were right, cuzzin'," Ace said in a phone call to Joker one evening. "Lotta old money here but I'm peepin' out a mix of poor white trash here who ain't so poor. It's blacks through here but I think it's only one family close to our new mansion estate that owns a mansion sittin' on twenty-five acres."

"A politician?" Joker guessed.

"Black hair care products mogul," Ace corrected him.

"Told you, nigga," Joker said conspiratorially. "It's Albanians hidin' out there controlling drug routes up and down the I-95 corridor, across to New Orleans. And they at war wit Hells Angels, Russian Mob, and the crazy mufuckin' rednecks in the swamp."

"And our biggest meth manufacturin' facility is now Jasper," Ace clarified. "Amongst all that mad shit you just described," he added with obvious doubt.

"Who put dis thing together?" Joker inquired in a sinister tone. "You or me?"

"You da boss."

"Aight den," Joker said, ending the call.

There was a section of the community named Briar Leaf Crossing, a known area of the community where outlaw bikers – primarily Hells Angels – hung out along with other individuals the local sheriff's department frowned upon but tolerated. The cops knew they were not the power-holders in the region and so they just fell in line like all the rest.

The good old peckin' order was at play in the Jasper region and Joker Red aspired to claim the number one spot in that order.

There was a large trailer park close to the sheriff's department. And many old low-income houses out there that had seen better days. They had a bar & grill in the vicinity with a small convenience store, post office, and a popular supply and animal feed outlet. Actually, it was the livestock outlet that had helped Meth Man Ace to make up his mind about settling on "the Crossings."

Ace had horses, cows, chickens, and goats. But one evening after he'd sent a truckload of supplies back to his mansion estate he'd made a detour. He decided to enter the bar that everyone in town frequented named Jenny's. Word had it that the owner of the spot (his name was Fat Teddy) – the deceased grandfather of Fat Teddy – had named an elusive swamp boar "Old Jenny." She was hard as hell to trap. Years later, when he finally was able to trap her, Old Jenny fed his family with her meat and fat for an entire Winter.

When Ace entered the bar he walked over to the farthest end from the front door and sat at the bar, waiting for the bartender to come over to him. He eyed her. She had no bottom to write a rap song about for the strip club but her thighs were thick. So was her chest. Her nipples were mesmerizing. Any man would look - even a child molesting, boy-loving, dirtbag, Catholic Priest. Ace guessed the woman to be in her early to mid-thirties at most. She had a long black ponytail that was coming apart. Her face was sweet, and she had a nice smile as well. She saw him looking at her.

"You're new around these parts," she stated conversationally, turning towards him, those two nipples aimed dead at his mouth. She smiled, and caught him looking. "Hello? I'm up here."

"Yeah…you're in both places. Can't help but see 'em." He was a tall New York City charmer and she loved the swag he had. Rolex Submariner, gold and diamond teeth, a million dollar gold and diamond Tony Montana – XL Cuban Link chain hanging around his neck with a piece on it that said "ACE" in all diamonds.

Ace was dressed in Valentino tan slacks, a white silk button-up, all-black Jordan sneakers, and a cool black Panama hat. Under the shoulders were fully loaded double Glocks, unconcealed, a permit to carry. He drew the eye of everyone inside of the bar in his direction.

There was a raucous crowd of around twenty-five drinkers. In the furthest corner of the bar were two pool tables and a cigarette vending machine. Ace counted seven redneck bikers - who likely were *not* Hells Angels - who inhabited the southern end of Okefenokee Swamp, which was a part of the new EIE methamphetamine mega-production plant at the mansion. They were living on his property like vagabonds. But he knew what they were really up to.

Ace looked back at the bartender. "Those the Duffy boys I have been hearin' about?"

She shrugged. "I don't -"

Ace dropped a $50 bill onto the bar and when she reached for it he sat his Corona bottle on top of it. "Talk. I don't fuck around. And I pay well." There was something icy and sinister about the New York bad boy.

"The two with the black hair," she revealed. "The others are cousins and friends of theirs."

Ace picked up his beer and she scooped the $50 up. Ace laid down another $100. She picked that up, too. He gave her his empty beer bottle and she discarded it. Moments later she gave him a fresh beer.

"You own that fruit and vegetable farm up the road in Jasper," she said. "What's your name?"

"Ace," he told her, displaying his military ID. "Army Ranger, chemical engineer, businessman."

She smiled. "I should let you drink for free for your service."

"No need," he waved her off. "What's your name?"

"Bonnie Blossoms," she beamed.

He removed a rubber-banded roll of cash from his pants pocket and held it up while glancing back over his shoulder at the Duffy clan once again. "Well, Bonnie, do you like money?" he asked.

She nodded her head.

"You'll be my eyes and ears, yeah?" he propositioned her. "And I mean I wanna know all the gossip, send me photos, let me know who all the dirty cops are – anything you come up with." Information was everything and nobody heard more than a bartender.

She nodded. "With how you pay, hell yeah."

"Free drinks on me Thursday thru Saturdays, seven to eleven o'clock for the next month," he told her. "Only tell the Duffys that it's from me. Who they tell is their business. Bill me. Tommy Cain AKA Ace."

"This place will be packed!" Bonnie exclaimed. "Will do. Every five hundred dollars on the tab you'll come and clear it?"

"Agreed."

He left a little bit after that.

CHAPTER 5

"Toenail Polish By Sephora"
Casablanca Hotel, Miami
<u>All Day</u>

"AAIIGH! UM! DON'T! WAIT!" Ciarán cried and moved back and forth. Her clit was being stimulated and she was loving the pain and pleasure but the panties were in the damned way as she rode on something like an inch and a half of that monster tool. "Ooouu! Oouuu! Shit!" Her vaginal tunnel was being stretched wide and sweet.

He wanted to stop her, but she had the perfect titties, and they tasted so good. He loved perky 32, 33, and 34-D cup breasts that were natural, and firm, had long nipples, silver dollar–sized areolas. Ciarán was a woman with a lithe tight body that she cared about and exercised. She smelled good when she got wet and started sweating because he had his face right there between her tits and under her chin, on her neck.

He thought of Tithi… and Romie and the heartbreak they'd caused. After Tithi, Joker decided to just focus on his wives. He lifted Ciarán off of him, kissed her up and down the side of her neck and began sweet talking her.

His hand was between her legs, and he was sucking on those beautiful titties. "Open up them pretty ass legs, baby…lemme see that wet ass pussy…wilder! Put them fuckin' legs up, knees back so I can see that pretty little asshole, too. Imma finger fuck it, okay?"

Ciarán moaned and played with her titties while he finger fucked her pussy and asshole. She got so turned on when he expertly tongued and licked her torso. She was so bad he sucked under her smooth pretty armpits, making her hips fuck and gyrate as he got her off with his hands only.

"Oh my God!" she gasped afterwards. "That was amazing!"

MEANWHILE, in their own room, Eustace "Bible" Reed and Charlotte Anders were lying down after relaxing in the hot Jacuzzi and receiving massages from two Korean women who worked at Casablanca Hotel. They had also stepped out to do some shopping.

She was wrapped in a fluffy red full-length terry-cloth bathrobe. She laughed at something Bible was saying.

"Bible noticed what?" she asked.

"Charlotte has perfect feet," he admitted as he lay next to her.

She sat up, sitting in the center of the large bed. She pulled off her big white socks. "What about them is perfect?"

He leaned up on an elbow. "Everything. They look small, slender, and perfect. They look…"

He shrugged, shy, which she thought was sweet.

"Bible Reed," she called to him.

"Hm?" He was staring at her feet. Tattoos were on one. Blue glitter toenail polish by Sephora.

"You have a foot fetish?" Charlotte inquired.

"For my woman," he stated with a smile.

"What do you think about doing to your woman's feet, Mr. Bibleman Reed?" she asked with a tease in her voice.

He picked both feet up and stared into her dazzling silver eyes. "Why? Are you gonna be my woman?"

She took a deep breath and wrapped both feet around his huge neck and ran her right foot along the left side of his face. As she played with him with her super-model-fine legs her robe flapped open. Flashing him what he thought was her bare pussy beneath the thick robe. She covered that buried treasure quickly, reflexively.

"Baby, I believe in *knowing*," she said in a soft purr. "When you know…you just know. There's no need to even ask. When I saw you in Chicago I just knew I wanted you. Now how about kissing them?"

Bible nodded and kissed each of her feet. "Your feet smell like a baby's. They smell good."

She ran her fingers through his short wavy hair. "Mm…the way you look at me makes me feel like melted buttercream on a white cake."

He sucked slowly on one toe at a time.

"Uhh, Bible!" she moaned as electric pulses of pleasure shot down into her breasts and through her moistening pussy. "My feet are connected to my pussy."

He first sucked her small big toe slowly into his mouth and slid his tongue between it and her second toe. "That feels so good!" she complimented him. "Lick the whole foot, honey. Mmm, yeah. It feels so good. Isn't it soft? Aren't my toes tasty, baby? Don't they taste sweet?"

"Mm-hm!" he nodded. "So white, so pretty, so sweet. Bible like lovely white feet."

He got into it, too. Her foot was so slender and dainty that he was able to put nearly half of it into his mouth at once. She loved it. He turned to her other foot and suckled on each one of her little toes before taking her foot into his mouth. She laid flat on her back and allowed him to have his way with her feet. Her pussy was so wet now.

"Bible love doin' this!" he whispered as he paused.

He reached onto the side table and drained one entire bottle of water. Then he pushed down the sweatpants bottoms he'd been wearing along with his Haines boxer-briefs underwear. She leaned up on her elbows and saw the big nine-inch bone swollen up like a thick foreboding cucumber, standing tall with tennis balls for nuts. In her mind, she was silently hoping that he didn't hurt her. Never had she seen a dick so long and thick.

Once Bible was completely naked she moved upwards to assist him in taking off her robe. He stood up on the side of the bed so he could take in her magnificent beauty. The breasts were about the size of apples but in excellent proportion to her tall frame. She had a pretty belly – it was flat and tight. The thighs were just right. Like her fabulous ass.

She also did her share of staring at him. Bible was 110% M-A-N like that Muddy Waters song. He was built like an NFL player and pro bodybuilder in one with muscles bulging everywhere. However, behind what he had was something more sinister and dark. She sat up but he moved forward, reaching for her hair, which was still pulled up into a cute updo, loosening it so that all of her lustrous dark tresses fell all around her face and shoulders. She let him open up her long legs and he dove in between them face first, noticing the gleaming juices that saturated her secrets.

Before he was even close to the pussy she was already dry-humping the air as if it was his face. She found his chocolate brown, mean-looking ass. She was never into small, yellow, slick-haired pretty boys and she could never relate to Latinos either because that wasn't how she came up. She liked them grimy, dark, and thuggish. Rough around the edges.

Her pussy was bald but she did have a few wispy brown curls at the top, above the clitoral hood. She felt his powerful hands grasp her ass from underneath and pull her off of the bed towards his face, which was covered by a sexy black beard and mustache. She observed him as he put his nose there… her wetness was everywhere! Her cream matted the dark curls she did have there. The labia and the white skin all around her wet visible pink, all looked like a paintbrush had been sloshing clear syrup all inside of that soft, precious area. He sniffed inwards as deeply as his lungs would allow. She wanted to see his reaction but she saw nothing. Only that he continued to smell her sopping wet pussy. Her steamy vaginal scent was awesome. She was fresh like a sliced mango.

However, she did see the way his body was turned as he lay there between her legs. He was turned some to the left, on his hip and left leg. She saw that his juicy black dick was hard as hell, like a kickstand on a motorcycle propping him up!

"Must smell like cake or somethin'." She managed to say and point. "My pussy smell turns you on, don't it?"

"You don't know?" he said. "It's sooo good, Charlotte! Sweet Charlotte. Your pussy smells *amazin'*! Bible wantchu bad."

He mashed his face into her and that's when the music got loud in her head and she couldn't turn it down. Didn't want to turn it down. Eustace "Bible" Reed knew how to eat a pussy like an Olympic pie-eating champion. And he loved eating the asshole, too. Now she couldn't wait to fuck that big cucumber-sized dick of his. Yolie must have taught him well. The man knew how to suck on a pussy and swallow her juices.

"Ohh, God, Eustace! Eat that pussy!" she cried out in pleasure. "It feels so good!"

He lifted his head, stopping suddenly.

"What?!" she whined in her sweet southern accent. "Why'd you stop?"

Her clitoris throbbed so wildly it was jumping.

"Nobody calls me Eustace, Miss Charlotte," he stated. "And I love it when you say '*my pussy!*' How 'bout you order me to eat your sweet asshole?"

She pinched her nipples and pulled really hard on them while giggling. "Stop teasing me, Eustace! Please?"

He pulled the hood back on her pulsating little clit, exposing the sensitive nubbin to the air. He kissed it and blew on it, teasing her and making her squirm, and pushed her vagina into his face.

"Eat my pussy, Eustace…suck my clit, big daddy," she begged. "You makin' me cum!"

She grabbed his ears and the back of his thick muscular neck, and her hips swayed and her asscheeks swirled her juicy slit all in his mouth as she creamed. Her body shook and shivered as if there was a cold breeze shocking her. She had a wonderful orgasm after being without a man for so long. *I think I had a real orgasm!* She thought.

"Okay, you big chocolate Incredible Hulk," she panted as she pulled him up to deliver the most sensual, wettest kiss either of them had ever had. "I needed to cum so bad and I think you made me have my first real orgasm!"

She sat him on the bed and they continued to kiss and hold each other. Her body was covered with a glistening sheen of perspiration which he loved because it showed how true the pleasure was. She caught her breath after a few minutes and kissed her way down over his massive chest.

"You are all solid man," she murmured in between kisses and love bites, "You great smelling man, too, Eustace. I love the masculine scent."

She made herself comfortable between his huge bulky thighs and grabbed ahold of his manhood. She twirled her tongue around the plum-sized corona and licked the salty-sweet clear pre-cum that had been drooling out of it since they had begun.

"*Mmwamf, mmf,*" she was saying or trying to say as she attempted to open up her throat and sword swallow his awesome size and length.

She had the most soft and full pink lips a woman could wish for. But her mouth was small on the inside. Nothing was wrong with that because not all men had horsedicks. Charlotte wasn't frustrated that she could take that huge, sweet man piece down her throat like those badass chicks do on some of those *ONLYFANS.com* and *PORN-HUB.com* sites she watched while playing with her pussy and asshole.

"I wanna swallow your cum!" she said after popping his shiny wet black cucumber out of her mouth. "Fuck my mouth! Nobody ever came in my mouth. I wanna swallow it. You taste salty and sweet… like a big juicy sausage."

She massaged his huge balls with her left hand. Her right hand was super-slick with the saliva cascading over his big, long dick, her hand, and his balls. Her head pumped up and down while all of her sucking, slurping, breathing, and moaning sounds filled their room.

"*Mmwamf, mmwampf, um! Ump!*" she went.

"Oh, Jesus! Oh so good! Uhh, yes, baby!" he was groaning, grunting, and moaning like a bitch.

Her head was going and his ass was lifting off of the mattress as he fucked his pole in and out of her sweet mouth. Her hands flew up and down as did her head. Then, from deep down in his chest, a whimpering cry originated.

"Mmmuuuaaiiee, mmmm! *Mmmwwaampf!* Mm, ggllrrbbb," she screamed when the gel-thick seed burst out of him and filled her mouth with a warm salty flavor.

She swallowed all of the sticky, squirting, and gushing man cream he had to give her. She nearly choked in the process. Bible was putty sixty seconds later as she let his still-hard pipe go.

"You okay?" she asked him as she climbed on top of him and reached for the bottle of water on the side table. She drank down nearly half of the one-liter bottle and he drank the rest.

"Bible," she murmured as they kissed. "Eustace '*Bible*' Reed."

"Charlotte Anders-Reed," he said back as she slid her wet clit against his long and thick slab of meat. "Mrs. Bible Reed."

His words were so intimate and sweet that they created an entire new pulsation of blood and heat to course throughout her body. "Damn, that sounds so sexy when you say it."

He maneuvered her into the spooning position and licked all along her neck, wrapping his huge muscular arms all around her. She felt like she was being cocooned at first by a python, but he made her feel protected as though nothing in the world could bring harm to her. One hand covered her right breast while his other lifted her right leg and he pushed the wide corona up against her tight elastic cavern.

"I hope it fits in you," he said into her right ear. "After Bible takes pussy, Bible wants Charlottes pretty asshole."

She shoved her creamy alabaster ass back at his hot penis and the juice that was leaking out of her lubricated him well enough to cause his big dickhead to pierce through her tiny cup-like opening.

"Aaannghnn!" she cried. "Take my pussy, baby. Then you can have my virgin asshole. You can bone my asshole until you scream."

He froze. "Bible hurt, Charlotte?"

But when she started pushing and twirling her ass back and fucking the two inches he'd put inside of her, he asked, "That means you want more?"

She nodded. "Yeah. Give me that big dick!"

Bible humped and pushed more of his massive meat into the beautiful silvery-eyed Cuban-American beauty. Each time more of his length went in, the slippier his penis became. Soon Bible was sliding nearly all of himself deep up inside of her.

"Umm. Eustace, feels so good, baby. I love it," she whimpered as she held onto his arms.

She turned her head around as much as she could to offer her lips up to her gigantic lover. He kissed as much as he could. The pleasure he was deriving from her lovemaking, how her wet pussy made him feel, was mind-blowing.

"Bible be yours, Charlotte!" he gasped.

She heard that and banged that pussy back harder. "You will?" He could even smell her breath and it was sexy.

"Bible loyal," he swore as she orgasmed so hard she bit his wrist. "Mm, your breath smells nice."

She wiggled away from him and stuck her beautiful ass up at the moon and laid her face flat against the pillow. "Fuck me like this! And cum inside of me. I wanna feel your hot cum splashing inside of my pussy." He could smell her wet sex.

He moved in behind her, found her portal, and re-entered the warm paradise of her body. He wasted no time thrusting and banging in and out of her. He treated her like she was the girl of his dreams and gave his soul to her.

"You like Bible's big black dick, huhn?" He manhandled her.

"Yes!" She loved the way he pulled her asscheeks apart.

"You wanna be fucked and sucked like them PORNHUB.com girls!" he said as he hit that little pink pussy harder and spit into her anus.

He slid his thumb slowly into her asshole and he couldn't take her sweet moans any longer. The sweat pouring off her body caused him to smell her wild Latina sex heat.

"It's gonna… oooouuu, Charlotte!" he whined, trying to control the pending explosion in his boiling nuts. "Want me to pull out? I don't want to get you pregnant!"

"Biiibbble! Lemme feel it! Cum inside me! I wanna feel your hot cum in me!"

He held on tight to her left asscheek while fingering her anus, and then he lost it. The explosion happened. She felt several spurts of cum shoot inside of her and she made sure she looked back at the pleasure on his face as her orgasm shook her to the core.

"You're up in my belly button!" she stated in disbelief as her face was planted flat against the pillow. "Stay deep inside me! Don't take it out…please don't remove that long black horsedick. Ohh, my fuckin' goodness… it feels so good. I've never been so horny in my ass or pussy!"

They collapsed into a hot, steamy sweaty heap of love and flesh. The entire room smelled like a feast of love. Soon, they were entwined in a soft, long, and loving kiss.

"I feel so open now," she murmured. "My pussy's stretched."

"That means?" he shrugged. "Bible don't know."

"A man doesn't understand," she said. "I haven't had sex in so long. A female's body needs to be watered like a plant. We're referred to as Earths by the Five Percent Nation of Islam. You ever hear of them?"

He nodded. "I'm from Brooklyn. That's where that all began. I'm surprised Charlotte knows."

She smiled. "And I'm from Decatur but spent a lot of time in Atlanta and Chicago. Anyway, a woman needs her man to cum inside of her. I'm so satisfied right now. You made me have my first *real* orgasm – several of them."

They fell asleep for hours after that marathon lovemaking feast they had.

CHAPTER 6

Tasha & Yolie Still Missing
The Palatial Mansion
<u>5:00 PM</u>

JOKER RED and Bible entered the palatial mansion a day and a half later and was happier than he'd ever been to see his wives and children. The only ones who weren't there were Uzenna, Leah, and Joker's older sister, Natasha.

"Where's my sister?" Joker asked as he was bull-rushed by all nine of his excited squealing sons and daughters. Each of the growing toddlers had their little hands up in the "raise the roof" fashion, wanting to be picked up. "All nine of y'all want me to pick you up?"

"Yes!" they screamed.

He held up the bags he was holding. "If Daddy does that, he can't give y'all the presents in these bags me and Uncle Bible got."

Hearing the magic word "presents" drove them insane.

"Well, you better enjoy them now, Red. Because we have nine more on the way," his blond beauty, Eden, mentioned.

Joker looked at his sexy wife. "Nine? Last I counted…Uzenna,

Coral, Ashley, Leah, you, Valerie, Iani, and Brittani make eight wives and I ain't been fuckin' no one else."

"*Cussin*, Joker!" Valerie admonished him. "They mimic every word they hear now."

"My bad," Joker said as they all walked into the children's playroom. He gave each of his five sons a gift to unwrap. "Where's Leah, Uzenna, and Natasha? And why am I having nine more babies when I only have eight wives?"

"Mommie have two more babies, Daddy!" His daughter with Valeria pointed at her mother.

"Ivory Brown Hodges! You told the secret!" Valerie accused the beautiful two-year-old.

"Oh! Mommie havin' twins, Ivory?" Joker picked the small child up and kissed her.

"She a snitch," Valerie said.

"Uzenna and Leah at the Central Intel Network and Tash flew up top," Brittani informed him as she and the other sister-wives helped the kids open their gifts. "We wanted to go with her because she said she was going shoppin'."

"Y'all know security's tight right now," Joker reminded them. "Who went wit Tash?"

Silence.

Joker shook his head.

"She can take care of herself, Daddy," Iani said to make him feel less worried.

"A lion can take care of itself, too, Iani," he stated, pulling out his phone to text his sister. "Until it can't cause a band of hungry hyenas."

Call me ASAP, his text to his sister read.

"You bought *drones* from them, Joker?" Ashley asked, sounding astonished. "They're barely even two!"

"Man, we flew *kites* back in our day," he shrugged as he spoke to the pretty brunette. "These kids nowadays…they sendin' tweets to the International Space Station and sh—*oops*. I mean *and stuff*."

"They callin' from Chi-town," Brittani blurted, trying to get a word in. "Nobody heard from Bible's girl, Yolie."

"We know," Bible responded. "We were lookin' for her and nothin'. Bible pray. Him pray now."

Joker looked at his wives. "See what I been sayin'? Not a one of youse is safe!"

"Are these things expensive?" Eden asked as they made sure the batteries were inside of the small drones. The women easily assembled all of the drones.

"Are you nuts?" he replied. "No. They're *starter* drones with like fifteen minutes of flight time before the batteries die. They're like forty bucks each so show them how to operate them. Then, as they grow older, they'll be better drone pilots."

Joker opened up another bag and passed out beautiful red velvet boxes with a gold silk ribbon wrapped around each one. Ashley, Coral, Eden, Valerie, Iani, and Brittani all squealed with delight and beaming smiles.

"What is it?" Ashley asked, shaking the box.

Iani gasped when she opened hers first. "Tiffany diamonds! I have a pink diamond tennis bracelet. Thank you, baby! Plus they're factory-mode *not* conflict diamonds."

The others had either a necklace, a ring, a small watch, an ankle bracelet, or earrings. They were all very happy.

Minutes later Joker was outside where they all tried to teach the kids how to operate the new drones. After a few dozen crashes Joker sat at the white wrought iron table with the frosted glass top. Charlotte and Bible could barely keep their hands off of each other as they took seats near the swimming pool on lounge chairs.

"Hm," Iani said as she poured Joker a whiskey on the rocks and passed out beer to Ciarán and Joker. "Who are you, honey? And why are you with our husband?"

"Ciarán," Joker said to his wives. "As y'all can see, Ciarán and her best friend, Charlotte, came with us. And I know youse are thinkin' straight from the gate that I *did* her. No, I didn't. Almost did but didn't."

Iani eyed Ciarán. "She's hot. It's been a minute since you brought us somethin' sweet home…so…" Iani shrugged, glancing lustfully between Ciarán's thighs.

"We definitely aren't mad if that's what you-" Coral began.

But Joker cut her off, saying, "I wasn't thinkin' that. They two decent women we happened to meet up in Chi-Town who were on their way to Atlanta…"

"Kingsland," Ciarán corrected him. "I feel mad awkward right now. I mean, you're a thick girl and I can tell you'd kick my ass for, um-"

"For wantin' some of Mr. Magic stick?" Iani asked with a relaxing smile. "That man could have Michelle Obama's pretty ass on all fours sobbin' wildly for more big dick in that pussy. We ain't trippin', girl. We ain't insecure. We're a sex family. We all love our man but its only one of him. The girls are plenty as you know. And then he meets people like you and…mm! Minds wonder. That's all. You look so hot."

"You like females?" Iani asked Ciarán pointedly.

"I've been with girls," Ciarán said as she clutched her beer. "Yeah." She felt her vagina clench and get wet.

Joker grinned and downed his drink.

"What the hell, Daddy?!" Uzenna said loudly as she and Leah stepped outside.

"What?" Joker shot back.

"Jackass don't know how to count," Leah said, eyeing Ciarán and Charlotte real quick.

"What da fuck is y'all two crazy bitches talkin' 'bout?" Joker demanded as Uzenna sat on his lap. They kissed like two lustful teenagers in the back seat of a car.

"First off, nigga, you said two days at the most," Uzenna said, checking Ciarán out.

"Turned into four," Leah said as she playfully slapped Joker in the back of his head. Uzenna did the same.

"Aight, Lee. Imma pick y'all sweet asses up and throw you in the swimmin' pool," he threatened them. He saw them looking at Ciarán. "This is our guest, Ciarán."

He finished his beer and whiskey and stood up.

"I'm horny as hell," Joker admitted, hugging Uzenna to him tightly, caressing her voluptuous buttcheeks underneath the cream YSL skirt she had on.

Uzenna got on her tiptoes to kiss him. "What about her?" Uzenna whispered. She knew right away that Joker didn't hit.

"She for y'all. I just want my wives," he told her as he kissed her soft neck. She smelled so good that he stuck his tongue out and licked her.

"Mm-oh! J.R!" Uzenna yelped, moving back. "And that other white chick all over Bible. Who is-?"

"Charlotte Anders," he replied. "It's kinda like it's a package deal. Charlotte's a Cubana-American. She clicked so well wit Bible after Yolie dumped him… I just liked 'em both."

"This girls from Chicago are callin' sayin' no one's seen or heard from her," she filled him in. "What's up wit Yolie, man?"

"Natasha, too," Joker stated. "I've texted her twice and nothin'."

Uzenna pulled him into the house, saying to Ashley, "Y'all betta give them babies to the nannies."

"C'mon, sister-wives," Iani said playfully as they picked up the kids and the drones. "Daddy's back and he's tryna lay out that pipe."

Ciarán just shook her head. Joker was rich. His wives were all beautiful. Especially Uzenna. She was just amazing to look at. Soon, the nannies had taken over the children and only Bible and Charlotte remained out there with Ciarán.

"Hey, sweet chocolate," Iani said as she sauntered back out to where Ciarán sat. Iani bent down and kissed her full open mouth-to-mouth for several moments. "If you want to, you can watch us. We'll take hours… upstairs master bedroom. The door'll be open, okay? I sure would love to suck your clit."

Ciarán smiled. "Okay. My goodness. My pussy would love it."

She sat alone in the chic patio area of the backyard. Bible and Charlotte had disappeared into the direction of the lake. Ciarán thought about Iani's sexy invitation and steam came from between Ciarán's thighs at the possibilities that lay inside of the Hodge's master bedroom.

Don't do it, Ciarán, a small voice inside of her told her.

What do we have to gain? Her throbbing clitoris returned.

"I'm so wet right now," Ciarán whispered as she walked into the vast palatial home. She passed by an armed female guard and stopped. "Um, Iani said to come… I mean…"

"Master bedroom?" La Colombiana asked.

"Yep, that's it."

"Take the elevator up one floor, walk straight to the end," Casci "La Colombiana" Caliendo instructed. "You and Charlotte have the guest room to the immediate right hallway when you get off the elevator, Brown Suga…if you like to freshen up first." Casci wanted to fuck Ciarán, too, but she was on duty.

Ciarán liked Colombiana. "Thank you."

Ciarán showered and dressed in a lavender and black satin short set. The top was a halter style with a deep plunging neckline, showing off her pretty brown breasts. She found the master bedroom, entered, and could not believe the orgiastic feast of love and carnal sex she was witnessing. Ciarán knew she was about to get more dick than she could ever handle and more sweet pussy than she could ever taste.

CHAPTER 7

Natasha's Phone Pings in BKNY
Central Intelligence Network HQ
<u>3:40 AM</u>

TWO MORE DAYS passed with no word from Joker Red's sister, Natasha. Worry was turning into anxiety, so at 3:00 AM on Thursday, Joker sat up and looked across the 17-foot by 10-foot Palace Bed he and all of his wives were in and tried to see where Leah was. She was usually either on one side of him while Uzenna was on the other as he slept in the center. But she was way on the other end still entwined with Apolina Noriega from last night's orgy.

His wives were insatiable. Ciarán was asleep there as well – for the second night in a row. The girls loved her. Joker could care less. He was done with other bitches. As long as his wives were content with him and what they were doing then he was content, too. Eight wives were more than enough for any one man to make love to regularly and he made sure he concentrated on bussin' each of them out every day or two.

"Lee," Joker called to her.

"Hm!" She was a light sleeper but grumpy when tired. "What's wrong?"

"Get yo ass up," he demanded.

She laid back down, her long blond hair covering her entire face and the pillow.

Ten minutes later Joker was showered and had a towel wrapped around him when he returned and yanked the blanket off of Leah and Apolina. "What'd I fuckin' say?" He spanked her bare white tattooed booty cheeks.

Leah had to climb over Apolina. She still had the dildo and harness on when she got out of bed, wrapped her arms around her man's neck and kissed him. Joker chuckled.

"Neva kissed a chick wit a dick before," he said, palming both of her phat jiggly asscheeks. She reminded him of one of those badass college gymnastics babes, except Leah had bigger breasts. She was a White girl trapped inside of a Black girl's body. "Put that thing away before you hurt somebody wit it."

"Youse a fool," she laughed. When she noticed the time on her cellphone she frowned. "What the fuck, Daddy? It's three in the morn-"

"Showered. Dressed. We goin' to C.I.N.," he told her. "My sister."

Uzenna heard them and got up. "I may as well go, too. All the noise y'all makin'. Soundin' like chickens cluckin' this early."

"I thought you had some bleeding, Ma," he sat next to her and brushed his wavy hair.

"I'm good. It stopped." Uzenna hurried to shower.

"I thought I was the only one who peed in the shower," Leah was saying as both women shared a laugh moments later.

Joker was back in the bathroom shaving his face of some stubble he felt there. "You bitches peeing in the shower?"

"I do it all the time," Uzenna said.

"Ew, Uzenna needs to drink more water, Daddy," Leah blurted. "Her pee looks like orange juice!"

Laughter. "No, it don't!" Uzenna was crackin' up.

"Fuck you, bitch, yo pee looks like crude oil!" Leah fired back. More laughter.

Twenty minutes later they were being driven in a new armored Mercedes Sprinter to the Central Intelligence Network building by Bible. Bushwacker, Casci Caliendo, Boo, and Divine came along armed with AR-15s and MP-5s, grenades, and Kevlar vests.

They went up to the fourth floor once they cleared security downstairs. Immediately, Joker started issuing instructions to Uzenna and Leah.

"Ping her phone first so we can try to get a GPS location," Joker ordered as he sat behind Natasha's desk. "I already checked her room at the Palace."

He looked at notes, and her desk calendar and cracked open her desk drawers. He was scanning everything looking for clues. He found a burner cellphone and checked the call log. There was only one number in it but Natasha probably deleted everything on a burner phone in the same way the entire organization was trained to do.

He called the one telephone number that was in the burner phone and it turned out to be Mecca Montecristo's Manhattan office number. Mecca was Joker's high-powered lawyer. No red flags there.

Joker knew that Sampson Gate, EIE's arms dealer, army builder (and more) liked his sister but Natasha was "slippery." She didn't hop from man to man. And she damned sure wasn't looking to be tied down to one either. She was like any other woman when it came to her sensual needs. But she didn't need to be in a relationship with a man for that. Natasha had a White "boy toy" stripper on call for that. He was pretty with blue eyes and long dark blond hair. His name was Daniel Fairchild and Natasha had seen him blowing up on Instagram, which had led her to his Onlyfans.com page. He was only 19 but so cute and the way he ate pussy almost gave Natasha cardiac arrest. He was hairless, damned near as pretty as her with no muscles. But women wanted him, his nice round ass, and that tongue of his went viral. His penis was six inches and super thick so he was perfect in that sense. Natasha also loved sucking it and his hairless balls.

But Natasha also had a real Black muscular man – all *MAN* – on call as well. His name was "Moss" and he had a ten-inch horse dick which he "sold" to her regularly. Moss was more than capable of using his piece on her like a whip to tame her and fuck her like Ving Rhames did to Tyrese's moms in the classic *Baby Boy* movie.

As for girls, Natasha was ultra picky because nowadays, bitches were nasty savages. All cute and innocent looking on the outside, but their houses were dirty as hell, dishes in the sink, beds unmade, sex stains from several different men on the *same* sheets, and God knows what STD these hoes were carrying and passing out like Halloween candy on October 31st. And then the ultimate disrespect: the prettiest bitches had no idea of how to get rid of the bad breath or the rotten onion aroma emanating from their pussies. A funky vagina could be smelled through jeans.

"Bitches are *savages*," she'd told Joker one night at a club in Miami. "I mean I love a clean pretty, disease-free, girl…*sometimes*. But they'll take cum shots and that shit turns to an ammonia smell because they ain't dealin' wit just one nigga. And they ain't douching it out. Then just because they're cute they think they get a pass. Bullshit. I can't stand cute plus funky."

"Yeah. Pass that shit up," Joker had responded. "Bitch got *shit* comin' outta her mouth and snatch."

"Exactly," Natasha nodded and laughed with him.

Now, Joker was emailing Lieutenant Gate:

I know you have been at the airbase in South Dakota but Natasha has been missing for several days now. If there's anything you can do to help us locate her, you know how to reach me. ~ J.R.

"Daddy!" It was Leah calling out to him from an office down the hall.

"Red!" Uzenna yelled as well.

He got up and hurried two doors down the hall from Natasha's office. "Whassup? What're y'all yellin' for?"

"The phone is pinging off a tower in Brooklyn right now!" Leah said, calling the phone on a CIN landline.

"It just keeps ringin'," Joker said, listening to it over the speaker-phone. "Where da fuck is she?"

"Report her missing?" Uzenna suggested. "To the FBI? Nina?"

"Back home," he ordered. "Let's go."

On the way back Uzenna reminded him of the houses that were being built for all of them. "Daddy, that construction is on a fast track and nearly completed," she informed him and pulled up new images on her laptop for him.

She revealed the new custom-built homes they'd been building on the 50-acre property on the outskirts of West Palm Beach and was impressed at the fast development. "Is that real fuckin' grass and flowers already?"

Uzenna nodded. "Yep. Fast-tracking means all hands on deck including the landscape architects."

"Y'all meant business!" Joker stated. "God! They done! What are they doin'? I don't see bulldozers, or backhoes, just vans and trucks in the aerial views. These are drone photos."

"Uh-huh," Uzenna said and showed him some interior video. "This is our house. The decorators are in there handling their business. All the stuff we demanded is getting done."

They arrived back at the Palace.

"How many houses on the Cul-de-Sac property over there? Eight just for us right?" he inquired.

"Twelve," Leah chimed in. "For security and EIE members," she added.

The sun was high in the sky by now. Joker turned to Leah and Uzenna saying, "Thank y'all for getting' all that done. I mean it's important to me because it's our safe sanctuary where our shorties can run around and not be shot or kidnapped cause we own the entire street, park, and so on. It's real big – I shoulda helped more. So…thank y'all. I couldn't do none of this without y'all at my back and side. Word ta da mutha."

"Aww," Leah and Uzenna hugged him in the foyer of the palatial home. When he spoke like that it made them emotional because it invoked pride.

Iani called them into the dining hall where breakfast was prepared. As always it looked like a King and Queen's feast. Joker laid several pieces of turkey bacon and jalapeno cheese slices onto a buttered onion bagel and ate with his family, including Apolina, Ariel

Montoya, Ciarán Hazlett, Charlotte Anders, Bible Reed, and all of the toddlers.

"Where's Rose Rice?" he asked, looking around. He was referring to Rose Rice Donohue, one of the three sex slaves, whom Bible and Nina Overstreet had freed from Albanian mobsters in Las Vegas several months ago. "And Kalani Muhammad."

"Here I am," Kalani murmured as she sat down between Valerie and Ashley.

"Rose is home with her parents," Eden said. "They kept insisting and the media started knocking so we let her go."

"C'mere, Kalani," Joker said to the beautiful 13-year-old light-skinned black girl.

Shyly, she came around the table and stood next to Joker. He kissed her cheek, pulling her closer to his side. "You good?" he asked her.

She nodded. "I'm fine."

"You need anything?"

She shook her head.

He dug into his pocket and selected an Amazon credit card. "You know what this is?"

She nodded. "Amazon credit card? You can order anything you want, right?"

"Yeah. Keep it," he said. "Order what you want but have it sent to your new address."

She was stunned. "New address? I thought you said I could stay with y'all as long as I want."

"Stop buggin' out. I mean where we movin' to, dummy," he said. He loved this little girl. Even after the hell she'd walked through there was this "real cool kid" sweetness about her that she grabbed a person's heart with.

"Oh," she said but he could see her pink lips still tremble a little and her eyes pool up a bit.

"You wanna be my daughter now? All of our daughter?" he indicated with a head swivel toward his wives.

"Do I call you Daddy?" she asked. "Or Mr. Joker?"

Joker chucked. "What do you like, kid?"

"Mr. Joker."

"I like that, too," he said, standing up and giving Kalani his chair at the head of the table. "It'll take some time but you'll be Kalani Hodges soon, okay? Sit here, kid."

She wrapped her skinny arms around him first and he hugged her.

"You gonna spoil that girl," Uzenna said.

"I spoil all my girls," he pointed out. "Everybody start packing up. We movin' outta this big ass monstrosity of a home. I'm 'bout to fly up to New York. Uzenna, Leah, please get Young Army here – now. Particularly my sister's sons. Smoke, Rome, and Brook."

"Got it."

Joker went to pack a suitcase and book a private jet to New York.

CHAPTER 8

Jenny's Bar
<u>Jasper, Florida</u>

AFTER METH MAN Ace's departure from Jenny's Bar, well after midnight sometime, bartender Bonnie Blossoms had pulled Joe and Roy Duffy to the side to inform them that Ace was covering their drinks.

Joe was a tall skinny man with black oily hair that fell to his neck. His older brother was shorter than him, carried around a beer belly, and was stout-looking. His face was pock-marked and his nose was crooked from being broken so many times.

"Free drinks," Roy spat. "Well, what the hell kinda deal is he up to, Bonnie?"

"Between you two guzzlers it's like hittin' lottery," she said, her voice dripping sarcasm.

Being that Roy was the elder of the two brothers he was the one who usually did the talking, and made final decisions.

"The tall, black city slicker in town you say?" Roy inquired, knowing her answer.

Bonnie nodded as she cleaned up behind the bar.

"What say you, Joe?" Roy asked his brother. "How 'bout we pay the rich city slicker a visit?"

Joe was apprehensive. "Let's run it by Pa first, Roy."

"I'm not sayin' let's start no trouble," Roy pushed.

"Anything you say, Roy." Joe didn't want to let his brother down.

In the end, the alcohol didn't win anyway. Both Duffy boys ended up falling asleep in their pick-up truck at the Okefenokee Swamp boat ramp at 1:30 AM.

The Jasper Estate

THE JASPER ESTATE EIE had invested in was best known for the sweet oranges it had produced over the years so that's what Ace and Joker wanted to keep it being known for.

"*EIE Farms*" hired a manager and general manager to maintain the lands and hired a discreet staff to look after the fruit and vegetable businesses. Ace hired mainly Mexican and Central American refugees who were most in need of the work.

The foreman's name was Estebán Esparza. Ace had hired him because Joker had told him to. For good reason. Estebán had twenty years' experience in running a farm in Texas until he was arrested for helping illegal aliens cross the border. He'd served six months in jail and found his way to Florida. Joker had met him while finishing touches were underway at the new houses being built for Joker's wives and children.

"Estebán," Ace said, shaking his hand. The foreman opened the door to his trailer to allow Ace entry.

"No, come on," Ace told him early one morning.

"Okay." Estebán walked out with Ace and saw a group of heavily armed men with him.

"Get in," Ace ordered Estebán.

A convoy of new SUVs and beautiful GMC pick-up trucks sped through the dirt roads that lead through the acres and acres of orange groves until they suddenly came to a stop. Ace and his men sprayed insect replant on their arms and other exposed body parts to ward off gnats and mosquitos.

"Rollo," Ace said to one of the hired security.

"Yeah, boss," the Latino man answered.

"Give Estebán a friend," Ae said while using high-end binoculars to look around them.

Ace had hand-picked most of his men but he also had EIE hittaz with him. Breach, Goliath, and Bushwacker were his security supervisors. Rollo was a Mexican friend Ace had met years ago while serving in the Army.

Rollo reached into the truck he rode in and came out with an AR-15. Ace took it, checked the clip, and handed it to Estebán.

"You can handle it?" Ace asked.

Estebán nodded. "I was in the Mexican Army."

"You ever kill?" Ace asked.

Estebán stared at Ace. "I use the gun when I'm ordered."

Ace stood there for a second and then smiled at his foreman. The eight-man group walked through the woods until they reached a boat launch and dock where Ace had several brand new airboats and a few other boats that were meant to get them through the swamp.

"All of my property lines are marked throughout the mainland and swamp land," Ace explained. "However, there is a … *faction* of meth-makers propped up deep back in the swamp. On EIE land. We goin' back here to exert our presence to these rednecks."

They unchained the boats, boarded them, and started up the loud engines. Ace let Bushwacker drive the lead boat and he sat beside him wearing black earmuffs. There were many canals and marshlands all over the vast Okefenokee Swamp. Ace knew that the swamp was not all of his so he stayed on EIE-owned land.

Soon, they spotted a houseboat where an entire family of White folks came out looking at the trio of airboats and gunmen dressed in camouflage shorts and T-shirts with Kevlar bulletproof vests on. Four of the ten family members were redneck men and one of them was on a cellphone. Ace pointed at the houseboat and the airboats stopped alongside the wooden deck built there.

Ace removed his earmuffs and observed the land that these people lived on. They had cows, horses, chickens, pigs, and at least two goats. An enormous 11-foot alligator was hanging from a cypress tree branch while two women skinned and gutted the animal.

"How can we help yuh?" a huge country redneck man asked. He had to be at least 60, thick white mustache and beard that extended down to his chest.

"Tommy Cain." Ace walked past him and two more young White men who held shotguns over their shoulders. "Y'all are trespassing on my land."

Ace saw the picnic table and the big turkey deep fryer they were using to cook the alligator. Ace walked out past the backyard area and looked at the gator, and the animals, all the while sniffing the air.

"Mah wife sure makes a fine meal, Mr. Cain," the family patriarch went on to say albeit uncomfortably.

Ace accepted a piece of the freshly fried gator hot off the barbeque grill and bit into it. The wife of the older man watched Ace blow on the hot Cajun fried meat and bite a piece clean off on the second try. Ace nodded.

"Good. Feed my men, too," Ace said more than asked. "What are your names?"

"They call me Old Man Duffy," the huge bearded man said. "Ah heard you knowin' my sons, Joe and Roy."

"Hm," Ace nodded as Mr. Duffy's wife, Barbra Ann, placed more alligator meat on the grill. "I know this and that."

The family was apprehensive about Ace and the group of killers he had with him. Soon, Ace and his men were eating alligator with rice and beans. The Duffys sure knew how to cook.

Ace got up to go as he wiped his mouth with a napkin. Old Man Duffy was baffled by the visit.

"Mr. Cain-" Duffy began.

Ace held up a hand. "Ace. Call me Ace."

"About the land," Duffy went on. "The last estate owners never bothered with us in the swamp."

"I own it now," Ace asserted. "That road used to access the boat launches is not public. And neither are the roads and trails through my orange groves where my foreman – Estebán – has noticed motorcycle tire impressions."

Joe and Roy showed up with a few male friends in a boat. They walked up to where Ace spoke with Old Man Duffy.

"Pa," Joe greeted.

"Roy, Joe, this is Ace Cain," Duffy introduced.

No hands were offered in courtesy.

"Why're you here botherin' my Pa?" Joe asked Ace.

"Shut up, boy!" Duffy barked.

"Listen to your Pa and have some respect," Ace told him. "Thanks for the meal, Duffy."

Ace started to walk off but stopped and turned back around. "I know what's goin' on."

Old Man Duffy had dead black eyes. Looking at him was like looking into a shark's eyes.

"Is that a riddle, son?" Duffy inquired.

Ace shrugged. "I saw the phone call come out…to warn all the others back further across the marsh and up the bayou. That's useless because we already know the dozen homes, shacks, meth labs…we know everything."

Silence.

"Okay." Duffy shrugged as he spoke. "Whattayu want?"

"Well, way I see it…" Ace proposed. "If we gonna be neighbors, may as well be friendly. Bring all your peoples over to the orange factory for a great big cookout. Then I'll let you know what I want."

Duffy saw no way out of it. "Can I say no?"

"No."

Ace and his men exited the premises at that point. As they got on the boat Bushwacker said, "I thought they was enemies, son."

"Nah," Ace told him as he put on his earmuffs. "It's bigger enemies out here accordin' to J.R. and that ain't them."

CHAPTER 9

"Ghostman Is Folk's Cousin"
The Tribeca Loft
New York, New York

AT JOKER'S BEHEST, "YOUNG ARMY" dropped what they were doing with Meth Man Ace's crystal methamphetamine production training and they caught a flight up to New York. Joker was already inside of the ritzy Tribeca loft he'd purchased for Tithi. At one point, he'd put it on the market but later changed his mind since he couldn't get his asking price.

Joker was alerted by the security desk downstairs that eighteen young men were calling on him. Joker cleared them to come up. Within minutes, his nephews were at the door: Smoke, Rome, and Brook. They embraced Joker and entered the lavish residence.

They were followed by the rest of "Y.A." members: Rampage (who was actually a butch female), Jimmie 2 Tymes (he was called that because he said damned near everything twice like that guy in *Good-fellas*), Mojo, Blood Money, Streetlyfe, Big Crip, Badman, Hop, Tip Toe, Grim, Broom, Budda Clips, Blue, Cocaine, and Crime.

The crew all had carry-on bags. Joker directed them into the living room where he already had weapons, communications equipment, and other tactical gear laid out over tables, chairs, and the floor.

"Nobody has been in touch with Tasha?" Joker asked the group. There was concern on his face. Anxiety.

"What's up wit our moms, yo?" Smoke countered.

Brook shook his head. Natasha hadn't reached out to any of her sons.

"We pinged her phone in New York," Joker informed them by turning a laptop around which sat atop a glass table near the arching exit. "Leah triangulated it right here."

"New Lots Avenue and Rockaway Ave.," Brook said aloud. "That's the Ville (Brownsville). What we got on Google Earth?"

Joker already had everything ready so he just showed Y.A. what he had. "While y'all look at that, lemme say this. Who'd snatch my sister up and why? There hasta be someone ignorant who did it because my enemies all know better than to fuck wit my family."

"Whatchu mean?" Rome inquired. Everyone was feeling anxious. Hearts were pounding, blood was boiling.

"Somebody in Y.A. got beef I don't know about?" Joker tried not to sound accusatory but he couldn't help it.

"You mean you think sometin' *we* did out here mighta got Momdukes snatched up?" Rome nearly exploded. "We been trainin'-for months!"

"He talkin' 'bout *before* we left, before we left," Jimmie 2 Tymes explained.

Joker walked over to the fully-stocked bar and grabbed a bottle of Grey Goose. He twisted the cap off, sat it on the blue marble bar top, and poured himself a double. He used the ice scooper to scoop up some ice, drop it in his drink, and replace the scooper in the ice bin. He splashed some lime juice inside his drink and carried it over to one of the large sectional sofas in the living room.

Joker cut his eyes across the room at his nephew. "No ones blamin' anybody for anything so watch how you talk to me, understand?"

Rome nodded.

"Everybody get a drink," Joker said.

Some of them just chose a beer from the refrigerator, others took the time to create mixed drinks. While they were busy doing that Joker opened up his expensive laptop and linked into an anonymous video chat with Leah.

"Hey," she was saying to test the sound.

"Whatcha got?" Joker inquired as he adjusted the audio on his end.

"I know where yawls at… but are we safe on this link, Daddy?" she asked him.

"I got Firefox running on private mode," he told her. "Plus a VPN service provider. But…two minutes and I'll be on TOR network."

Leah cut the link and waited. The laptop Joker had was not encrypted. Leah, Uzenna, Iani, and the others who worked inside EIE's Central Intelligence Network were all hyper-aware of how vulnerable communications between two computers were. How easily "private" messages, text, and even video conversations could be hijacked.

"Whatchu doin', Unc?" Brook asked Joker.

"Guaranteeing myself strict anonymity, Neff," Joker replied. "When fuckin' wit these devices people like us can't be sloppy. Y'all listenin'?"

Young Army gathered around where he was sitting on the horse-shoe-shaped sectional with the laptop on his lap.

"Take the terms 'PRIVACY' and 'ANONYMITY' for example," Joker taught them. "We got Firefox running from home with a direct connection to your ISP, right? You don't want nobody pokin' their noses in so you select 'private mode' tab in Firefox, okay? This disables cookies – and doesn't allow your computer to store any remembered websites, search history, nothin'. But this privacy is limited. It doesn't do shit to prevent the IP problems. Internet Portfolio. Google, Yahoo, Bing…The ISPs literally sell everything you type to these tech giants for their *laser-targeted advertising* schemes which are worth billions. Google can find out where you live, who your ISP is…"

"Google Earth Maps," Brook mentioned.

"Uh huh…" Joker got onto the TOR network better known as the Dark Web which he was familiar with. "The tech giants can see it all. Ya girl can't, others in your house can't, but the tech people can.

Anonymity is what takes privacy to a different level, where anything you do online can be hidden behind layers and layers of digital barriers. That's where TOR comes in. The Dark Web, which gives you privacy and anonymity unless you holler out details of who you are, the city you live in or the state."

"That'd be ridiculous," Rampage said. "If you gon' be that dumb just go on to One Police Plaza and turn ya'self on in."

"Hold up," Joker said to them. "You there?"

It was Leah again. He could hear her but couldn't see her until a few seconds later.

"Your sister called," Lead told him.

Joker sat forward, his heart leaping at hearing that piece of information. "What? So that's good."

Leah was eerily quiet.

"That's good," he repeated. "Right?"

"I don't know," Leah said. "You know Folk?"

Joker's heart turned to ice at what she'd just said. "Folk? *F-O-L-K,* Folk?"

"Yup," she replied.

Joker paused. "What she say and how'd she sound?" His undertone was obvious worry.

Leah said, "I recorded it. Listen…"

Moments later:

Natasha: *Zenna?*

Leah: *No, Leah here. Tasha?? That's you, Tasha?*

Natasha: *I really gotta talk to Joker.*

Leah: *He think somethins happened to you. What the fuck, Tasha? Where are you? Are you safe? Tell me what's goin' on and he'll be on it. He already on it.*

Natasha: *Some crazy, crazy shit went down and I need –*

Suddenly, Joker's sister's voice was cut short and it sounded like the phone had fell out of her hand. However, another voice came on.

"Hello?" a man's voice said, commandeering the phone. He had a Western Indian accent. *"Whappen, star? Where da Red Mon?"*

Leah: *"Who's this?"*

The man replied, *"Folk. Jokah Red Mon, heem know, star. Let da bredrin know me soljah in da hood made monsta mistake when dem not know who dem took."*

Leah: *"Folk...put Joker's sister in an Uber and let her go and that'll be that. This is some real serious shit already."*

Folk: *"Me know. Red Mon a rootless bad boy killa. Big big mistake made, Mon, and GLP not wan' war, seen? But Folk like mek shur seen?"*

There was an audible *'click'* that signified the end of the recording.

"That was it?" Joker demanded. He held his hands out, dumbfounded.

"Yup," Leah told him. "You have EIE security here – at CIN - that say they know Folk. Who da fuck is *Folk*, Daddy, and who's *GLP*? It's not clear on Google except for…the Gold Lion Cub?"

"Golden Lion Posse," Joker filled her in. "And Folk a dirty killa, a former cop from Kingston. He a wolf. And GLP has an army. A rogue army of dirty cops."

Rome, Brook – all of Young Army – were all ears.

"We know the strip club Gold Lion," Rome said, realization coming to his face. "And the name Folk."

"These niggas comin' outta left field fuckin' wit us," Brook said. "I'm worried 'bout Momz."

"Cats who know me don't make no mistakes like this," Joker stated.

"Wassup?" Leah wanted instructions.

Joker scratched his head. "We gotta fuckin' issue…That goddamned Ghostman is Folk's cousin. And I thought Folk had gotten deported but…he has more power now. And people."

A resounding silence followed that admission because Joker had executed Ghostman for betrayal. Now a powerful ally of his had emerged from the woodwork.

"Shit," Smoke uttered.

"Guess he had the right name, huh? Cause just like a ghost, dat mufucka comin' back to haunt us all," Joker nearly whispered the foreboding comment.

"She aight tho, Uncle Red," Brook said, not truly confident in his declaration.

Joker had Leah play the call back. Afterwards, he was convinced that Natasha was in grave danger.

"She may *sound* aight…" Joker trailed off as he packed a carry-on bag with weapons and another suitcase with an expensive sniper rifle system inside of it. "But that's cause she had a gun to her head…or they just treatin' her aight - for now."

"Plus, she looks very good," Leah reminded them. "I mean she's stacked, very pretty. If I was a man… and wanted to…"

Joker glanced at Rome, Brook, and Smoke. "Okay, Leah, we get it. Let's get ready to roll out."

Joker looked at Leah on the screen.

"Whatchu need me to do?" she urged.

"You know where you triangulated her cell?" Joker started.

"Yeah."

"Can you get a scan of every cellphone in that same area in the past forty-eight hours?"

"We can do that," Leah assured him. This meant that every live cell phone that pinged off of the same cell towers as Natasha's in that triangular area she was last thought to be in would be captured and printed out on a spreadsheet. "But it's New York City so we can easily have tens of thousands of numbers to sift through."

"Hm," Joker mumbled. "That WNBA contract you bein' paid ain't enough?"

"I got this, Daddy," she said. "What am I lookin' for?"

"*Ethan Clay*, AKA Folk," Joker instructed. "Anybody named Clay. Start at Golden Lion Night Club."

Leah shook her head. "Clay's a common name but we'll see if we can get a number on him or one of his immediate family members. That's what you need. And he's a business owner so…lemme see what I can find."

Joker nodded. "Wife, son, mother - that type of thing. A daughter won't be important to him."

"Bastard."

"Yeah. Most important get me something specific," he told her. "Let's see if we can turn up a location, an address other than the nightclub."

They ended their call.

Joker made one more call on a burner phone. "Bible?" Joker said when someone answered.

"Boss!" Bible's voice breathed hard into the phone. "W-why, w-what, what Bible do?" he stammered out.

Joker shook his head. "Let that girl go for a minute, son," he ordered with a chuckle.

"Charlotte, stop," Bible whispered.

"Okay look," Joker ordered. "Folk from Brownsville got my sister. She alive."

"Bible come now, boss," he said. "What else?"

"I need a plane and helicopter at my disposal here in NYC and all hands on deck," Joker directed him. "The base will be back on the old block – Fulton and Willoughby."

Brook clapped his hands hard one time and exclaimed, "That's right, Uncle Red! Back to them Brooklyn streets goddamnit!"

"THE INFAMOUS GOLDEN LION POSSE: ALL KILLERS, VIOLENT HITTAZ, AND NARCOTIC TRAFFICKERS."

The way to battle two powerful serpent such as a Burmese python or the Black Mamba (or any venomous enemy for that matter) is that you cut off its head.
Such necessary destruction is not Chinese arithmetic.

-Bashar Al Assad,
President of Syria

CHAPTER 10

Folk's Story
Origin of the Golden Lion Posse
(GLP)

JAMAICAN-BORN KILLER ETHAN "FOLK" Clay was a notorious Brooklyn Kingpin who operated from out of the Brownsville section of Brooklyn. He was not a big man in stature but his character and name were bigger than life. He had grown up on a hardcore block in Kingston, Jamaica, with a strict father and mother who'd kept him in school.

He'd been recruited by the Jamaican National Police. It was from there that he had learned that being corrupt paid a lot more than being an honorable cop. For nearly twenty years he'd gotten away with accepting bribes from some of Jamaica's most feared narcotics smugglers.

The dirty Jamaican cop was – or had been – assigned to the Notorious "Dark Leopards" which was an elite Major Crimes unit. Two years after Ethan Clay had made it into the Dark Leopards they had executed a night-time raid on a farm in St. Andrews Parish that had been owned by one of Jamaica's most dangerous drug bosses, Martin "No-Finga" Carpenter.

Ethan had tipped No-Finga off that the raid was imminent. Ethan had been promised $50,000 and a new house if he could help stop No-Finga from being captured. At the time No-Finga had nowhere to run because the Dark Leopards had the main roads out of No-Finga's neighborhood blocked.

"Have ya rude boy nem start shootin' immediate as we come, seen?" Ethan had ordered No-Finga. "Me tek dem wit me, dem go down."

What Ethan had done was kill his own squad inside the police van he had been transported in. He'd used two 9mm handguns that were non-police issued to do the brutal *"insider killing"* of his fellow cops. But they were all cops he did not like. No love lost.

He had forced the driver onto No-Finga's farm where the National Police had knowledge that No-Finga had cocaine, heroin, and mari-juana bound for the Bahamas and the United States – along with some of his Colombian partners who'd been illegally staying in Jamaica under No-Finga's protection. As soon as the lead police van had been spotted by No-Finga and a group of his henchmen they'd opened fire on them.

Ethan Clay had shot the driver, shoved his body out onto the ground, and jumped out of the van. He'd run over to the other van where six more Dark Leopards were taking cover behind the vehicle. They'd had no knowledge of what Ethan had done.

"Ceasefire, star!" Ethan yelled as he held up an AR-15.

The six men had followed his commands and as soon as they did Ethan had looked at all of them and ruthlessly mowed them down with lethal .223 rounds from the AR-15. Moments later No-Finga had come down the gravel-covered driveway, literally smelling the gun smoke.

"Bloodclot, mon!" he had exclaimed in disbelief.

"Ya g'wan kill me…or use me, star?" Ethan had asked.

"Me word is solid, star, like dem bullets nem in da blood clots A-R, seen?" No-Finga had answered him. "You me folks now, seen?"

Ethan had nodded.

"Your name, star," No-Finga had inquired as a dozen of his killers encircled them.

Ethan had shrugged. "*Folk*, seen? Juss call me Folk and me ansa to dat. Me like it much, star."

"What we need?" No-Finga had pointed at the two vans and the carnage.

"No-Finga," a muscular Jamaican man had called the enormous No-Finga over to the van Folk had arrived in. Folk could see the missing middle finger on No-Finga's right hand as he smoked on a cigarette. The man was huge. At least 300 pounds.

"Jah Rastafari!" No-Finga had a cold look on his face as he inspected the bodies. "Folk."

Folk went over to where he'd been standing.

"Me have anotha farm in 'aint Elizabeth's Parish," No-Finga had started instructing Folk on what to do. "Ya police chief been comin' hard on me people dem, seen? But dis is a massive *murda* dem! Bad Boy next dem send a strong army of fifty. So me give you men…seen? All dis must disappear. Right now, you go! Drive one, dem drive the otha. Go! We clean up da scene. Move out, star!"

"My pay," Ethan had said.

"Me know where you live," No-Finga had told him.

Folk had nodded and he'd driven one of the vans – after all the other bodies had been loaded into the second van – off of the St. Andrews farm. They had stripped the bodies naked, meticulously chopped them up, and had them burned for eight hours inside a sawdust and wood pile that was soaked with gasoline. The vans were taken to a junkyard owned by another crime boss and ally of No-Finga where they'd been melted down.

Before he'd left he had called into the National Police Headquarters to report that while on the way to the raid, the squad had been ambushed by a gang of masked assailants and he'd been held at gunpoint. He'd claimed that they were all tied up, blindfolded, and driven into a wooden area in Spanish Town.

"Me shot!" he exclaimed. "But me escape bad man dem. Wait! Wait! Me tink me see dem-"

He'd looked at one of the Columbian hitters and said, "Tek me to Spanish Town and shoot me."

And that's exactly what had gone down. He was driven out to Spanish Town where he'd urged the two men to beat him, shoot him, and make it "look good." The two men busted up his lip, broke his cheekbone and jaw, knocked out several of his teeth, cracked his ribs, and left him in Spanish Town. He'd rolled around on the muddy ground and started walking until he noticed a convoy of cop cars racing past him. He'd managed to wave them down in the torrential downpour.

The National Police, Jamaican Army, and police from several parishes had joined in the search for all the other "kidnapped" policemen. Folk had maintained from the outset that after the ambush, the 13-man Dark Leopard squad had been bound, gagged, tied up, beaten severely, and transported to Spanish Town. When Folk was pressed about the whereabouts of the others he could only say that he'd escaped from a moving black van after he'd wiggled free of his binds and blindfold. The others who'd tried to escape had been recaptured, but he'd outrun them.

National Police Chief Lance Van Horn had wanted to know if it was No-Finga and his men who'd been behind the kidnappings and Folk had said none of the masked men had dreadlocks, none were Spanish, and they looked like trained professionals.

"Rebels? Military?" Van Horn had been baffled.

Folk had been released from the hospital and had returned home. There he'd been visited in the middle of the night by one of No-Finga's men who had handed him a black canvas gym bag. Inside of it, he'd found $50,000 along with the title to a brand new Audi and a deed to a house in Montego Bay.

"No-Finga keeps heem word, star," the henchman had said. "Heem need yuh back at da National Police, seen?"

Although the investigation dragged on for months, what had mystified police was their inability to turn up a single body. The public had been outraged, family members were emotional, politicians were making the most of it, and the media had circled around the story like hungry sharks. The case had eventually went cold after a year.

No-Finga sicked Folk onto all of his competition. Folk had eventually risen to a position of power within the National Police when he'd taken over the Narcotic Unit as 1st Lieutenant. He commanded a squadron of his very own handpicked men. Sixteen brutal killers had been put through the Academy by No-Finga and trained by Folk to work inside of his unit.

They shook down anyone not connected to the No-Finga crew. Folk had gone after all of the big-time cocaine, heroin, and marijuana dealers. Specifically, he'd been interested in eliminating the Colombian cartels who'd been using the island as a transport hub for their product to be launched closer to the USA – such as to the Bahamas – or transported directly to the USA by various modes of transportation.

Folk's narcotic unit had become a brutal shakedown and kill squad. Not only did his crew take what they could from the cartel suspects, but No-Finga had no problem with giving them suitcases stuffed full of cash to keep them happy.

A decade later Folk had made all of the right connections with Colombian cartels, the Venezuelan military, and everyone else he needed to move his show on the road. He already sent a dozen of his men to Brooklyn to open up The Golden Lion strip club. Each of those men had been Jamaican National Policemen with esteemed records and all the right credentials that came with it.

Over a period of 18 months, Folk had flooded Brownsville, Brooklyn, with a hundred men who would become the infamous *"Golden Lion Posse."* All killers, violent hittaz, and narcotic traffickers. The most frightening part out of all of it had been the fact that the Golden Lions were all dirty Jamaican National cops who'd entered the United States *legally*. Folk had been an evil, calculating, and sophisticated man. He insisted that each of his men enter the U.S. for "good reason" to justify their visa: aviation school, forensic studies, sniper school, U.S. National Guard, NYPD Police Academy, etcetera.

"Tink da long game, star," he always pressed upon his men. "We slowly go to New York and tek ova, seen?"

Folk had amassed a respectable $2.5 million he'd kept hidden in the Cayman Islands. He had stayed behind in Jamaica with his crew as they cleaned the house. They murdered No-Finga and all of his closest henchmen…and women. They stole all of his narcotics, his cars, his jewelry, and even a small airplane.

Folk had managed to produce to his National Police Captain a taped conversation where No-Finga was drunk and boasting about: *"Me kill dem blood clot National Police, mon! One night, star, a dozen gone!! Me snap me fingah and boom – gone, star, seen?! Don't fuck wit me!"*

Folk had "roped" him into saying it and No-Finga had finally put the nail into his coffin. But Folk – as dirty as a cop as he was – he was no fool. He'd concocted a plan to kill…to assassinate No-Finga, steal his riches, massacre his cronies, and when it was all said and done, then *and only then,* produced the recording to top officials inside of the National Police Department.

By the time Folk had come to the United States in 2009, his plan was well underway. He'd signed up for the U.S. Army Reserves at age 30 but was later medically discharged due to the bullet still stuck in his left shoulder after the "kidnapping/murders" of the Dark Leopards where he'd escaped. Folk was the owner of the Golden Lion Night Club in Brownsville. He had an effective lawyer and CPA, who made all the right moves to obtain Folk's licenses from the SLA (State Liquor Authority) and everything else the Golden Lion needed.

The Golden Lion Posse had its base of operations, plenty of men (some of whom were on the NYPD now), and guns and drug connections directly from cartel producers in Colombia. The Golden Lions were solidified in Brooklyn and had been since 2004 – years before Folk himself had arrived to sit in his New York throne.

Joker Red and most of his original Everything is Everything network were aware of Folk and his goons. The GLP, essentially, was a vast mob of rogue cops who'd wormed their way into the United States from out of Jamaica.

What Joker wondered was, why now? Why would GLP and Folk put their necks out on the woodblock now? Vengeance for Ghostman?

Whatever reason they came up with…no one got away with fucking with Joker's family.

Somebody had to pay for that shit.

And God forbid if Natasha was harmed.

NYPD connection or no NYPD connection, there would be assassinations of cops all over the city against GLP's rogue pigs. Joker never had any problem with taking out a cop.

He just hoped his sister made it out okay.

CHAPTER 11

WITHIN THE NEXT 24 hours the apartment building still owned by EIE, Inc. on Willoughby Avenue was teeming with throngs of EIE mercenaries. Thankfully, the four top-floor apartments were vacant and Joker Red's uncle, P-Man – which means "Dopeman" in that old New York "slang" – ran the pool hall; he'd left it in the hands of his family members who were never part of the "bigger picture" Joker had put into motion in recent years.

"Red!" P-Man called out to him as Joker and a group of EIE hittaz stood in the hallway talking.

P-Man was a clean-cut, 6 foot 2 inch, dark brown, 59-year-old Black man. It only took one good look at him to see that he kept himself in good shape. He'd never been in the military or anything of that sort but he had served seven years in the feds during his twenties. Since then he'd steered clear of cops, rats, and courtrooms. He still believed that crime pays but a criminal had to choose one type of crime and then firmly stick to it. There was no way to master them all.

No way to be as master of all of them. It only took one time for

P-Man to get burned and he'd changed his whole tune. He kept the dopeman moniker ("P-Man") but he never again touched the stuff. He had noticed what Joker Red was doing and when his niece, O'Mira Dukes, had asked if he was interested in managing the Jamaican Restaurant space, the pool hall, and apartment building for a nominal salary - $20,000 per year – P-Man had agreed. However, he had asked Joker Red to set him up as a gun dealer. Joker had hooked him up with Lt. Sampson Gates and P-Man had never looked back.

"Yeah, Uncle P," Joker acknowledged him.

P-Man wore an expensive silk two-piece suit which was charcoal gray, made in Italy. He had black leather Jordan – Mids on with a gray NY Yankees fitted cap. He was fresher than crisp cold lettuce with a $50,000 Hublot watch on to top it off.

"Ya phone keep buzzin' on the table over there," P-Man told him.

Joker hurried on over to the cherry wood coffee table where he'd been sitting a few minutes before. Joker flopped down on the sofa and checked through his missed calls. He noticed that Leah had called him three times from a burner phone that was not connected to EIE's Central Intelligence Network (or "CIN").

He returned her call. "Why you ain't text?" Joker asked after she answered.

Leah ignored the question. "You asked us to get cellphones that pinged off of cell towers where we last pinged her phone. Daddy, the spread sheets a mile long but out of over fifty thousand numbers that hit off of that same triangle of towers within hours of Natasha's last ping, we have two hundred people named Clay. Nina Overstreet called Verizon Mobile/New York and they pinged a '*Victor Clay*' at cellphone number 347-215-0807. He is the *son* of Ethan Clay and Victor's a NYPD who's posted out of the 1-0-3rd."

Joker saved that phone number in his phone and said, "The hundred and third precinct is in Queens. What the fuck is *Officer Friendly* doin' in Brooklyn?" he stated sarcastically.

"You also wanted addresses other than their notorious Golden Lion Nightclub," Leah went on. "Check ya text messages."

"Mm huhm, I see 'em," Joker told her. "This Victor Clay?" He had to cough lightly to clear his throat.

"Yup and a woman in Long Island," Leah informed him. "Melba Clay. We can't confirm if this is Folk's wife, daughter, or what. He's nearly sixty, a strip club owner, he probably likes 'em young."

"Why? How old's the wife? Or this Melba?"

"Twenty-seven."

Uzenna could be heard in the background saying, "The daddy thing is in. And him bein' a powerful man... I can see it cause it makes the best sense. Young chicks love forty-, fifty-, and sixty-year-old men. They're master lovemakers...and callin' 'em Daddy rings so true."

"Malek and Nina are both trickling over a lot of information about Folk," Leah informed him. "Check your TOR link. Did you know about the details of this man and his crew?"

Joker stood up and thrust one hand into his black Levi jeans right front pocket. "Anybody in Brownsville heard of 'em. They ain't no friends of mine but the GLP is notorious."

Leah paused for a second. "Baby, the Armenians were one thing -"

"*Albanians*," he corrected her.

"Whatever. This is different," Leah stated worriedly. "These bastards have the attention of Interpol and DSS."

"Diplomatic Security Service?" Joker's face turned agitated suddenly. "DSS? What da -. Who said that?"

"Malek," Uzenna said.

She meant Special Agent Nyomi Malek of the FBI.

"I really didn't want CIA and FBI knowin' what's up. Not wit this," Joker mentioned as he fired up his laptop. He logged in and found the TOR link Leah had sent to him.

"I know," Leah and Uzenna both said.

Leah mentioned, "He has an elaborate setup. Cops on the force he owns. That fucker is as dirty as the ocean floor, Daddy. In Jamaica, when he was National Police, an *entire* drug team he was on went missing, and are presumed dead. He was the only one left livin'."

"He'd suffered a non-life-threatening gunshot wound and was beaten up pretty badly," Uzenna added. "Social media thinks he did it."

"I'm on the Dark Web – lemme get back," Joker said to them. "I'm readin' everything now. Tell Malek and Overstreet that I got this."

Joker called out to Bible and moments later the huge dark herculean man walked through the front door.

"Yeah, boss?" Bible replied.

Joker wrote down the TOR link and gave it to Bible. "Has everyone read what Leah put on the Dark Web about the Golden Lion Posse? There's shit in there we ain't know about them."

Bible Reed knew that the situation was dire and that as brave as Joker was he could barely hide the fear and paranoia he was feeling in his heart and stomach for his sister Natasha.

"Boss?" Bible put his humongous right hand on Joker's left shoulder after the colossal beast of a man sent out a group text to the EIE Army.

Joker looked up at Bible. "What?" Joker answered.

"Permission Bible speak?"

Joker nodded as they stood face to face.

Bible sat next to Joker on the sofa? "Bible commit acts Bible think unforgivable. Do you believe God will forgive us for what we did?"

"For the United States or…over there?" Joker countered. "Cuz if youse talkin' 'bout what we did over there we're doomed, Bible."

"But the Lord says -"

"*I KNOW WHAT HE FUCKIN' SAYS!!!*" Joker exploded out of nowhere, his demeanor popping from zero to eighty in a flash. "LOOK!!" he shouted, spittle flying from his mouth as he pulled out a small handheld black book which had no writing on the outside of it.

"Is that a Holy Bible?" Eustace Bible Reed inquired.

P-Man had re-entered the room at that point.

"Yeah," Joker stated. "I read it…page for page, back to front, creation to Revelation!"

Many EIE henchmen had heard Joker – a usually laid-back man – explode and they'd come into the apartment to see what was going on. Not only that but they had gotten the intel on Folk…

"You were baptized into Christ and those sins you fear that doomed you were washed away and forgotten by God," Bible told Joker.

"Even what we did over there," Joker said more than he asked. "I mean Afghanistan, Tunisia, Syria…"

"I know what you mean, Bible remember it," he said.

"Do you?" Joker doubted it due to Bible's brain injury.

"I remember," Bonecrusher added.

Joke took a deep breath and looked over at Boo who was clutching a water bottle. "What about you?" Joker inquired.

Boo shook his head and pulled out a small Ziploc bag with a dozen or so different pills inside of it. "Percocet, Xanax, Adderall, Celebrex, Abilify, Neurontin, Bushbar, and some other shit. I'm a man with PTSD, paranoid schizophrenic, depression, suicidal, and homicidal urges every day who wishes to kill the president and my wife. Ain't no God gon' forgive us for killin' babies, their fuckin' moms, and participating in that black magic ritual shit with those… Devil demon bitches."

Divine suppressed a laugh. "You mean the witches' daughters?" he corrected.

P-Man gawked. "*WHAT?!?* I never heard that one. What da fuck?"

"Our platoon was caught in a fuckin' once-in-a-century downpour…flash floods and mudslides never seen before in the Jebel Chambi Mountains," Divine recalled. "We had a humanitarian mission to deliver UN supplies to the government. That storm was catastrophic."

"A real shit show," Boo stated. "Our drop point was in Tunis but we were ordered to Kasserine. We took cover from the storm in what we thought was a hostel or somethin'. Turned out to be the home of the town medicine woman."

"*The Kasserine Witch*, they called her," Divine informed P-Man and several EIE who'd never heard the story. The apartment's living room was now packed.

Young Army was, particularly, all ears. Joker was tuning them out as he read what Leah had sent regarding GLP and Ethan "Folk" Clay.

"She was beautiful," Divine continued. "And I mean *bad*. Them Tunisian women is somethin' I'd never known were so damned pretty."

"Tunisia is what – Asia?" Smoke guessed.

"North Africa," Divine told him. "Way fuckin' North Africa. Them niggas ain't dark like mufuckaz in the Congo, Chad, Kenya, or other parts of Africa. Tunisians is bleached niggas…Anyhow, the house was decent and filled with women. At first, we thought they were all daughters of this beautiful woman called *Mircalla*. They all wore hijabs and veils. We *thought* they were wholesome Muslim girls."

"And?" Brook probed.

Divine looked at Boo and Boo shrugged.

"I thought we wasn't gonna talk about what we did over there," Bonecrusher interjected with concern.

Divine had a cynical smirk on his light-skinned face, "They fed us, let us bathe, drink their wine and liquor, and they disappeared. Late into the night they believed most of us were too drunk to rise. I went into the kitchen, hungry as all hell. Boo, Red, Knarf, Bible, y'all know all who was there that night. We were all thinkin' food and just hopin' for some of that pussy runnin' around under that mufucka. I hear music first so I go to find it. They got these downstairs layout sofas all along the walls, a wooden floor like a dance studio, and Mircalla's out there *bone naked.*"

"Yeah? Everything out?" Smoke was grinning wickedly.

"Well…they were all naked but *painted*," Boo told them. "Their skin looked airbrush painted so perfectly."

"Tribal colors," Divine said.

"*Tribal* colors?" Boo stated disagreement in his voice. "Black and white body paint on all five of them. Mircalla was older than the other four but not old. She looks like the porn bitch SaraJay Camsoda in a way."

"She do," Divine agreed. "Especially dem titties."

"And these bitches had *hijabs* on?" Rome asked. "I thought they were Muslim."

"We thought the same," Divine said. "But this Mircalla had drawn out this Satanic circle in the center of the floor and they had hundreds of candles lit all around. They saw us and didn't even blink. Incense was lit and each girl began to chant as they started to do this ancient ritualistic dance. First, they pleased Mircalla with the most sensual of massages, they kissed her, fingered her, used strap-on dildos on her, then on each other…that was the first night."

Boo picked up the explanation from that point. "Business as usual the next day. Hijabs, prim and proper women. A bit later that night the mudslides still had us closed in so we told the base that we were still stuck but safe. No body paint but there was powerful witchcraft, chants they showed us how to do with them, and blood sacrifice."

There was a shift in the room. And silence.

P-Man stared at Boo. "So what y'all had to do to get some of that pussy? Cut your hand and drip some blood in a cup? Or cut a cat's throat?"

Joker walked back in, having heard enough. "No cats, no hands."

"Boss, I wasn't gon' say…" Boo stopped him.

"Why da fuck not!?" Joker snapped coldly. "Y'all in here tellin' it while Tasha in danger…so fuckin' tell it all, nigga! We was *mesmerized* by dem Tunisian bitches. Satanism, witchcraft…we watched them slice the neck open on a virgin – killin' her – and *we all drank her blood.* The wild shit is Mircalla was the mother of the four younger ones."

"Wait, what?" P-Man nearly choked on his beer. "She was having lesbian orgies wit her *daughters*? Where was their father?"

"Never asked," Boo answered him. "Prolly got sacrificed."

"Y'all started fuckin' 'em?" Budda Clips asked.

"How old was they?" Mojo wanted to know.

"Mircalla was still in her late thirties," Divine said. "The four daughters between eighteen and twenty-one I'd guess." The revelation left them stunned.

The entire group studied the GLP files after that.

Not too long later, Joker gathered up his army of killers.

"Melba Clay is in fact the new wife," Joker told the dozens of mercenaries as they stood inside of the spacious living room. "Bonecrusher, Ceasar, Breach, Boo, Knox, and Blackout… go on out to Long Island and snatch her up. They have a toddler – take him, too, but don't harm 'em. Leah and Uzenna will have more intel for y'all en route. Stay in full stealth, silencers, face masks, etcetera. Y'all know tha drill. Take her to the warehouse."

Once that team was gone Joker looked at Divine and said, "Ethan Clay's brother at the Hundred Third -"

"I thought he was the son," Divine corrected.

"My bad." But Joker was just testing Divine to see if he was on point.

"C'mon, boss, nice try," Divine smirked.

Joker nodded. "You right, kid. Victor Clay. Sweep his ass up, too. Don't hurt him. Remember, he's a NYPD and we gon' need him back alive for Tasha. Take Darkstar, Starscream, Barricade, and Goliath. Wait 'til he get off and he by himself. Masks, stealth mode, etc. Leah gon' steer youse right to him."

"Warehouse up Otisville?"

Joker nodded.

They exited.

Bushwacker eyed Joker. "What we gonna do, boss? Wait around for them assholes to get back?"

Joker shook his head, a sinister grin on his face, "Nah. We ridin' out."

"Where to?" Bush wanted to know.

"To da Golden Lion strip club," Joker Red told his men.

Bushwacker nodded. "Fuckin' right, nigga! Yo, yo, yo! Loud ass niggas!! Da boss said we riding out to da Golden Lion!"

It got silent suddenly.

"Bring the ghost guns in case we need 'em," Joker ordered. "The hardware we'll leave in the trucks cuz they have metal detectors. Let's ride, E-I-E."

"We rollin'!" Bushwacker led the way.

CHAPTER 12

Sleepin' Wit Da Enemy
Ethan Clay Estate
Valhalla, NY – 10:00 PM

FOLK STOOD at the mouth of the high-arching mahogany wood doorway leading into the living room, watching Natasha Catherine Hodges sitting with her legs crossed - staring back at him. Folk was sharply dressed in a tailor-made suit by Valentino. It was all gold as though he were about to host the *BET* or *THE TRUMPET Awards*. A red silk tie by Gucci, a white shirt by Kors, and black Gator shoes. Presidential Rolex, an all-diamond chain and bracelet had him looking like Ziggy Marley or Gucci Mane 2010.

"Flashy man," Natasha stated. "Gold agrees with you," she complimented him.

Folk's face was clean-shaven, his eyebrows a thick black without gray in them, but his dreadlocks were salt and pepper. He had a hair-stylist who kept his hair clean, shiny, and stylish. They were presently inside of his mansion in Valhalla, New York – near White Plains.

"You like it?" he asked her as he laid a white box down next to her with a red ribbon tied around it.

"You'll look good buried in it," she stated cynically.

He scowled and walked over to the bar where he mixed apple martinis. "You tink me fear deaf, star? Me live the lives of a *hundred* blood clot dem, seen?"

"This shit is tirin', man," Natasha told him with her arms crossed in defiance. "You need to let me go."

"Has anyone hurt you?"

"Not physically but I'm bein' held against my will," she reminded him. "There's that... but I *knew* you, so..."

He brought over the tray of drinks and sat them down on the expensive frosted glass coffee table. He handed her a martini and they clicked their martini glasses together. They drank simultaneously and sat the glasses down on the coasters he provided. Out of his inside jacket pocket, he produced a red rectangular box.

She looked at him and then back at the box. "Folk, what are you doin'?" she questioned him.

"Me neva ordah me men to tek yuh, seen – one hundred percent *mistake*!" Folk stated. "Meh need yuh to explain to yah bruddah dah error, seen? *No war*. But, next ordah of bizness...you are one of the most beautifuliest women in the world and me wan' you gul, seen? For a long time me saw and me heart bang, bang..."

"Lemme text my brother I'm okay, Folk before you get people killed," Natasha warned. "And if you talkin' some *whore* shit I'm no whore. You said *next order of business*. We can talk business but whatchu doin' is *dangerous*. That whatchu want? Fire burns."

Folk waved her off. "Meh know Jokah 'ave massive and cruel army of killa mercenaries, star. Meh 'ave massive army in da street and NYPD, star. Me no afraid of no one, seen? Howeva...me wan' you. No intention of harmin' you. So text him. Please, mon. Mek it cleer."

Tasha accepted the burner phone Folk gave her and sent Joker a text:

Bro, I'm straight where I'm at. I haven't been harmed. I don't believe Folk even gave the order. Some of his ambitious men tryna earn points when they saw me alone. Folk wanna "talk biz" (e.g.,

fuck). I'll holla back. Lemme have time to pick his brain. Stand down.

She showed him the text before sending it and he smiled a mouthful of platinum teeth on the bottom row.

"You're a cynic, eh, star?" he asked as he removed the SIM card from the phone. "Smart and cynical, mon."

Natasha knew that she was a badass bitch. Having Joker Red as her brother gave her a unique brand of power even over other powerful men like the one who sat next to her. But, after GLP had pulled this bullshit, Natasha wondered if she was talking to a dead man. Joker and EIE didn't need much of a reason to knock some heads around. Them niggas were "hunters" for real.

"Open the box, gul," he said, laying that O.G. Jamaican game on.

She looked at the box sitting on the sofa between them and placed it in her lap. First, she removed the top and then she moved away the thin paper lining. She giggled and pulled out a black party dress by Prada. It was a high-end special edition fashion showpiece priced at $10,000 and Natasha was impressed.

"I mean…" She was gushed while standing up and holding the dress to her curvy bombshell body. "I know the cash is nothin'. What I like is you actually picked my size. I'm flattered."

She kicked off her sassy new black Vera Wang high heels and his eyes fell to her narrow feet and her freshly painted powder blue toes. Her legs were as beautiful as the rest of her but she had the feet and toes of a foot model. Folk had a profound foot fetish and it took all of his willpower not to ask - - no, *beg* – the beautiful creature to let him fall and allow him to worship and lick between each toe. He *yearned* to suck them.

Natasha walked down the hall and into the bathroom. He followed her. She didn't close the heavy door behind her. The sexy hazel-eyed woman slipped out of the dress that she'd been wearing and stood there clad only in a black G-string and see-through lace bra.

He watched her put the dress on before he walked into the bathroom. She was staring at her own fascinating figure in the mirror and eyeing him as he eased up behind her. He put his hands on her hips and eased them slowly around the front of her soft, almost flat, belly. Her faint shampoo scent mixed with perfume made him dizzy.

"You are a cold, bloodless man," she said in a soft voice. "But the way you look at me makes me melt."

He knew how to use his hands. Although she'd been seeing Lt. Sampson Gates from time to time it wasn't regularly. Like most EIE women, brutal and violent men with true power was what made her feel alive. Dangerous killers and psychopaths turned her on and made her want to suck their dicks…like having a craving for sweets.

Folk reached underneath the dress and cupped her G-string covered pussy.

"*Cold and bloodless?*" he murmured as he licked her ear. "Dat what da gul like? Ya pussy drippin' troo da panty, mon! A blood clot watah common is down here, seen?"

She pushed him away. "You have a fuckin' wife, huh?"

"Damn," he murmured. "Tro da cole watah in me face, seen? Dick *big bone* hard!"

She slipped back out of the $10,000 dress and watched him eyeing her beautiful asscheeks. Secretly, she *loved* that he had a wife. Forbidden fruit made men as hard as granite.

"You sixty but youse a sexy ass Jamaican nigga," she told him while reaching behind her to see how big his manhood was. "*Oh. MY. GOD.*"

She pulled him back out into the living room and pulled down his underwear, releasing his pipe. She sat him down, on the sofa she'd been sitting on before, and suddenly – out of nowhere – she shook her head.

"Uh, uh, Folk," she said, shaking her head. "First…you have a *giant* dick. And my coochie's small. But women dream of pieces like that. It's like a black pipe bomb."

She reached down and lightly stroked him with her left hand and weighed his bulky scrotum with her right. Pre-ejaculate was already bubbling and streaming out of him and cascading over her hands. He smelled very clean which she liked. Them O.G. old-head dudes were "O.C.D." about their hygiene. They knew the ladies found that attractive. He smelled like Blue Nile Muslim oil. But there was something she was checking out about him – in infinite detail – that she didn't like.

"Wah'pen bad gul. Kiss me," he asked.

"Uh-uh. You have too much hair there," she pointed out, still stroking him sensually up and down. "I admit, you smell nice and make my pussy wet. But the hair…"

"Ok." He entered the bathroom and exited nearly a half hour later. He had used a cream depilatory on his lower parts, re-showered, and rejoined her in the bedroom. "Come."

She shook her head and smiled. "You so crazy. Whatchu do?"

She sat next to him on the bed, let him grab her around the waist, and feel her up on her ass while his robe fell apart, revealing his bare naked, pulsating, penis and huge scrotum. Not one hair in sight, which *made* her want to be an instant dick-sucking slut. But she didn't, which was the 100% #1 reason why White women were winning the "Game of Sex" when it came to Black men. A White bitch would've swooped right down on that delicious honey bone like it was nothing. What did Natasha do? She reached inside her purse for a tube of cocoa butter-cream and squirted it up and down his muscular quadriceps, his arms, legs, chest, and especially his hard, veiny, dick and balls. He was so hard.

He sat up while she gave him the best hand job ever and stripped off all of her clothes. Soon her bare pussy was exposed and because of her steamy moist female arousal, he could smell the pungent scent of her coochie even more. They both became hornier and hornier as time went on.

Folk pulled her warm lovely body closer to his own, kissing her sweet juicy lips, sucking and nipping at her neck, and he was making her want to plant that pussy on top of his manhood. It stood up so hard and so big. He kissed her like she was a Telemundo soap opera star like Carmen Aub or Karla Carillo. She had to stop for a second because there was too much feeling, too much passion and emotion behind his tongue-sucking and lip-biting French kiss. *Christ, my pussy is way too wet!* she was thinking. At least she was trying to think but she was also cloudy. A bit confused. His men had made a bad mistake by snatching her up. Supposedly made a mistake.

"Hold on, Rasta," she said after another delicious squeeze came from Folk's hands. His right hand had found its way into the warm cleft of her ass. Her slippery pussy cream lubed up her hairless asscrack and when he touched her tiny anal opening, she undulated her bottom, wanting to be penetrated up the anus because her clit was ready to explode from the pleasure build up. She also loved to have her asshole licked, fingered, and fucked.

"Wait…w-wait!" she demanded, his eyes on her widespread caramel-honey-colored thighs. She watched his nose twitch and flare as he inhaled deeply. She was able to discern right away that he was smelling all that wet pussy nectar spread out like lotion between her legs and her crotch areas. *God, he was such a nasty freak,* she thought.

"What, sweet girl?" he asked.

"So, you're sayin'…" she paused before re-asking the question. "Am I kidnapped?"

"Me tole ya no," he said while simultaneously shaking his head and staring at her lovely big breasts. He leaned forward. "Me g'wan suck dem titties. You 'ave beautiful, bountiful, titties!"

"So I'm leaving right now," she told him.

He froze. "What? *Leave*?? Why gul?"

"If I stay and we fuck, won't that be rape?" she took on an innocent quizzical tone. He was slobbering all over one breast, squeezing it as she laid back thoroughly enjoying his masterful breast play.

She had both of those lovely light brown legs busted extremely wide open with her knees back. He was out of his robe and on top of her butt naked, his johnson looked rock hard and mean. He held her gorgeous titties together like two scoops of his favorite ice cream and started licking and eating.

"Rape?" he said lustfully as he bit her left nipple, swirling his soaking wet tongue around and around her dime-sized areolae. Then he did the same thing all over again to her right nipple and areolae. He was making her so horny that she was feeling like her pussy was about to cum in squirts without him even touching her down there. "Me da candy man and heem 'ave nevah no need to take it."

She smiled and he returned to kissing her again. Each suck of her tongue sent chills down her back. His rock-hard Mandingo piece throbbed against her Venus mound in the area right above the clitoral hood. As soon as she felt his heat, her naked pussy humped up and down against the fat dickhead and wide underside of his horny, hard, and hot length.

He looked down at her gyrating hips. "Look to Folk like freaky Natasha 'wan be raped by me big sweet dick, huh? You like?"

"Fuck! I want that Jamaican rude boy dick bad as hell!" She was swirling those hips and bumping her clit up and down, sideswipe, side-swipe, sideswipe, and then up and down as if her pussy was placing a wet kiss on his tip. "My, ohh hell yeah, Folk. Fuck me, Folk. Stop teasin' me!"

He flipped her over onto her belly and put several pillows under-neath her. He spanked each bouncy cheek.

"Ow!" she giggled playfully, reaching back to rub the area where she was feeling the sting from the slap. It felt hot…and so sensual that it caused her clit and cuntlips to swell up with the kind of blood that shot straight through the genitals.

"Yah say rape? Okay, so I said no rape! Now yah get a sex spankin' fuh dat," he admonished her.

Her beautiful round backside squirmed and tried to get out of the way of his hard spanks but **SLAP!**

"Ouch! Mm, shit it hurts!" she whined.

Smack! Slap!

"Oh shit…yes! Fuck yeah! Spank my ass!"

Slap! Slap! Slap!

Her pussy was leaking like a faucet onto the pillows.

"I'm so confused, Folk." She toyed with him while looking back to see the expression on his face as she wagged her fine asscheeks in his face. "Because you say I'm not kidnapped. And my pussyhole is sopping wet… in need of a good Jamaican fucking. But if you fuck it…"

She reached back with both of her well-manicured hands and inserted a finger inside her pussy's entryway from underneath with her right middle finger. She could still see his eyes watching her and it was a turn-on. She sucked on her left thumb and fell to her right side. She used that moistened left thumb and pushed it into her asshole. Folk watched as Joker Red's sister Natasha see-sawed her fingers in and out of her body. In a couple of minutes, she was on her back finger-banging herself with two fingers in the pussy and two way deeply buried inside of her ass. She was sweating and her musky sex juices were bubbling out everywhere like a glass of tea and honey was tipped over onto the floor!

Folk grabbed her from around the hips and she grabbed him by the head and the dreads while shoving all that "mushy-gushy" wetness into his face. He got right up in between that wet slit and ate it like she needed it to be eaten. She was a wild sexy woman, too.

"Mm, suck that honey, baby!" she stated sluttishly. "Get all that honey up outta there, Folk."

He nodded, looking at her as she face-fucked him with her sex. She was shoving her pussy into his face, riding his nose like it was a dick. She was so turned on, hot, and horny that millions of goosebumps could be seen on the surface of her skin. Her nipples stood up like nine-millimeter bullets on her big firm titties and small rivers of perspiration fell like rain over her beautiful even toned body.

Folk put both of his big palms underneath her big lovely booty and spread the halves apart. This way, her small vagina opened up somewhat. He leaned back and kissed her asshole as if it would kiss him back. In a way, it did because she let loose a small fart, which was perfect timing because it opened a tiny bit to let in his saliva-soaked tongue. His thumb pressed and massaged her clit and everything seemed to relax and open for him. From the vulva to the labia minora (the two thin inner folds of skin) and then on to the labia majora (the two outer folds) – and down into her anus. The woman was sort of like a flower that opened with moisture and sunlight from the sun. Only Folk was doing the opening. The kissing, the licking, the loosening…

"Aaaaiiiieeee, ooooouuuuuuu, shhhhhhhh, cumminnnnggg, Fuck!

Fuck! Fuck!" She whined and shimmied her asshole and pussy all up and down his face, very, very, close to squirting a *rainbow* of hot stored-up girl cream in his face.

"Don' move gul.. Folk take it now, seen? Heem take what heem wan!" He ordered her to stay still. He held his big brown menacing "man-bone" out towards her and she watched as he buried the huge poker deep inside of her hot squishy baby maker.

As soon as he was inside of her he sank it in until his big nuts hung over her, still lubed up, lights out. She grabbed his back and scratched the hell out of him making him bleed.

"Brooklyn, New York City Gul 'ave da bes' pussy in Jah's Great Kingdom, mm, mma-ma, blood clot, pussy dem B-K gal nem, star!" he was grunting, kissing on her, and squeezing her phat tits, going mad inside of her.

"Say it. *Say it*. I wanna hear it, Folk!"

Now he stopped banging her pussy out because he had the wild female lion eating out of his palm. This pretty mothafucka was purring. She was tamed. She was still leaving that tight wet thang upwards and fucking the shit out of his oily dick. Her twat juices had him lubed up so good.

"Turn flat, gul," he commanded her.

"You want my ass?" Her eyes got all big.

"Yah! Turn and me say so," he promised in his accent.

She turned and lay flat.

She also reached back and pulled her wet asscheeks open. He pushed his huge dick deep into her backside and within a minute, he was boning her little asshole like they were *Lexington Steele* and *Pinky XXX* making a porno video.

"This what you wan'? How yah wan' be raped?" he asked as he licked her right ear.

"Uh-huh. I have *'rape fantasies'*," she admitted while taking the dick like a pro.

"*Fantasies* is more dan one," he pointed out.

"I want multiple men to fuck my slutty pussy and I want my mouth to be fucked like a hoe until he cums and makes me swallow," she admitted.

She made his dick even harder talking like that. He suddenly started hammering her hard and deep. He was on the verge of nutting…

"Okay, I'll rape dis ass!" he almost yelled and then he squeezed her ass super tight as his big balls let loose everything they held inside. His breathing all but stopped as his hot, sticky, globs and globs of semen.

CHAPTER 13

The Folk Estate

<u>Valhalla, New York 11:00 PM</u>

"BE BACK." Natasha was still laying under him when she felt his dick was still hard inside of her rear end.

She wiggled out from where he had her pinned and that's only because he wanted to keep stroking. She showered with him and they made love again. "You on Viagra!" she said afterward.

"I'm not… only wan' on something." He chuckled as they got dressed.

"Who me?" she pointed at herself. "Only time I fantasize about bein' raped is when I'm on Henny. As any bitch. That Henny sex may be mixed wit a lil perk or zannie. Oh yeah, I'd want *rough* sex, period. Oh, Monday – or a boring day – no sex at all. Clean da house, go shoppin', throw on da lingerie, spray on that Dolce and Gabbana *Blush,* hair done, feet and fingers done, and smoke wit my man, feed him and suck his dick real good. I love suckin' a hard, big dick."

"No pussy? No ass?" he asked. "You no wan' cum?"

"This coochie and bootie gotta sleep, too, baby," she reminded him. "They need rest."

He ensured that she got her belongings back after he put the finishing touches on getting dressed. He had her sit inside the living room while he collected the video footage he'd secretly made of them having sex. He hadn't figured out what he planned to do with it yet.

"You ready to ride out?" he inquired of her.

She nodded and minutes later she followed him out of Folk's ritzy Valhalla estate. They were ushered inside of his sinister black Maybach which was operated by a well-dressed armed goon. There were three other BMWs for the security team that he rolled with.

Destination: Golden Lion Strip Club.

Blindsided by the Butcher
Golden Lion Strip Joint
<u>Brownsville, New York – 12 MN</u>

"Damn Brooklyn has changed!" Satzi exclaimed while she hopped out of the blue level 5 bomb and bulletproofed GMC Yukon Denali. Several other women were with her and they were all connected to the EIE mercenary group. Satzi was the wife of Boo who was one of the top mercenaries.

Along for the mission was probably the most lethal weapon inside the EIE arsenal Casci Caliendo – best known La Colombiana – followed by the Polynesian bombshell (Zaza), then the Afghan stripper (Citra), and the sweet yet edgy, Ariel Montoya who Bibleman, Joker, and Nina had freed from the Albanian's sex trafficking ring in Nevada. The "weapons" – well, the *women* – were parked in a quiet obscure, location next to Brookline Hospital in Brooklyn.

Shortly after they'd arrived, some ten blocks away, a large 18-wheeler was parked in East New York. The huge $150,000 Kensworth was idling next to a warehouse with its trailer doors opened. Two ramps were put down and one by one the EIE came zooming out of there on various kinds of fly gleaming black motorcycles. Within minutes the killaz pulled up and stopped in the parking lot next to Brookline. Two luxury Sprinters were there with Joker,

Bushwacker, and some others. Joker got out of his vehicle and walked up to Satzi.

"Here's the Sprinter remote starter," he said, his eyes falling on Ariel and wondering if she was cut out for this. "Do I need to worry 'boutchu?"

She embraced him, pecked him on the cheek, and whispered, "You keep lookin' at me like I'm a baby. But it's okay becuz you're my Papi now…After all this is over I wantchu to make me yours. I masturbate every bath I take cuz I saw how you fuck."

He kissed her lovely-shaped mouth once and seeing how soft and sweet she tasted, he French kissed her, not caring who was watching. "Yeah, we'll see, baby," he told her. "Ari, you ride wit Satzi up to Otisville and wait for my call or text. Go now. Boo's at the warehouse."

He watched Ariel turn to leave. She was wearing a mad fly bright yellow feminine hoody cut over her pretty, flat belly and the sweat pants that went with it designed by St. Louis rapper *Quille* owner of TRAPWEAR, LLC. One of them is BMF Record Label Boys. Ariel was killing that joint the way her succulent asscheeks filled that suit act. The men were all staring.

Bushwacker whispered. "Her booty crack must be hungry the way it's suckin' dat fabric all da way up in it, huh J.R?"

"Word," Joker smiled.

"Boss, wassup wit it?" Bone inquired once the girls peeled off. "We out in da fuckin' open too long."

"We still got other cars," Joker told him, glancing at the time on his Hublot. "Plus, Bibleman pickin' up Apple, Carla, Izzy, Gates, and Junga."

"Tasha is Gates' lady, huh?" Bone threw it out there.

Joker nodded. "That's what I thought, yeah." And then he pointed. *"There."*

Bible arrived in another bombproof SUN – a black Cadillac. He had ditched the rental vehicle at the storage facility where Joker had the armored car stashed. Then he'd headed out to La Guardia Airport where he'd scooped up Carla, Isabella, and Apolina (Apple).

And Lieutenant Sampson Gates. They were happy to see him because it was getting cold and windy outside.

Then two more Sprinters appeared, loaded up with even more EIE mercenary personnel. Apolina and the other ladies were nervous. They didn't know all the scary details, or the frightening history, about the Golden Lion Posse nor their tight connection to law enforcement in the city.

"Boss, um…" Bible stammered but Joker was not being attentive to him.

"Everybody load up!" Joker ordered as a call came through from Leah.

"We about to roll," Joker told her. "What now?"

"Man, listen!" she snapped. "He tryna call you, motherfucker!"

"Imma fuck you up, Leah," he warned her for popping shit.

"You ain't doin' a damn thang," she taunted him courageously.

"Who is it, Folk?"

"Yeah, goddamnit."

"I ain't havin' my GPS pinged," Joker informed her. "Put him through to burner three."

He powered up the new burner and waited for Leah to connect the encrypted satellite call. It took a few minutes but when the phone rang Joker answered the first ring.

"Aight."

"You 'ave meh wife, star!" Folk growled into the phone. "An' ya 'ave meh son! Meh fust born! Meh say dat ting wit ya sistah was a mistake and dat meh mek it right witchu, star. What way we go 'wan wit it, seen?"

"Nigga." Joker looked at the phone like somebody coughed Corona 19 into his face through it. "We waited for Tasha to walk away free since it was a mistake and she didn't. That's where da fuck we goin' wit it! Where the fuck is she?!"

"Meh 'ave her in da car wit me, blood clot boi!" Folk declared. "We goin' meh club right now, seen? You nevah should have touched meh fam, star. Yah sis right here! We like each one of us more dan yah know, seen. Ask da beauty Queen Natasha Caterine Hodges if meh lie, star…Meh not lie. Word on Jah.”

Joker was like: *What this mufucka say? I know he ain't say what I think he said.*

“We ‘bout to tear dis mufucka up,” Joker whispered. He told Gates, “Get da MK-18 deployed out back and two 50 calibers out front on…”

Gates pointed, “Denny’s Restaurant rooftop.”

“Do it,” Joker ordered. “Apolina, Carla, and Junga… go get eyes.”

Joke kept up the conversation. “Put my sister on. I’ll ask her, star.”

“Bro!” Natasha started. “Y’all snatched his wife and kid? Maaan, cut them loose.”

Joker shook his head. “Shut up. You don’t know a goddamn thing ‘bout this gangster life. You’re dead. You hear me? *Dead*. Da second I let them go, **you’re done**… are you understandin’ me? He seduced you and prolly banged you cuz it’s a mind game. A *dick trick* dummy. Cuss me out if you understand.”

“You’re a fuckin’ asshole!” she snapped.

“My peoples just walked in Apple, Carla, and my mans,” Joker stated. “When the mufuckas start screamin’ you *run*.”

Leah was sending Joker live video from inside the club which – via her amazing hacking skillz – had picked up through Apolina’s rigged-up cellphone. Joker looked at his laptop. All of a sudden Folk excused himself to greet a big, dark-haired Italian man. Joker froze at recognizing him.

Vinnie the Butcher. *What the hell's he doing here?* Joker asked himself, astonishingly. He picked up another burner and called Carla who was sitting next to Apolina in The Golden Lion. “Ayo, Carla…is dat Vinnie Braga in there? Talkin’ to dat yo-yo?”

“Yeah, nobody had a chance to talk to you,” Carla stated. “I don’t know the whole particulars but he’s out here pointin’ fingers about Jessika Cicero.”

“Tell Apolina to put her phone more towards them and while he got his back turned, get Tasha’s stupid ass outta there,” Joker ordered.

Carla walked to the table where Tasha was and made a head gesture while saying, “C’mon girl!” And the two ladies walked out onto one dance floor. Junga stood up and popped first one then two smoke cannisters and walked away, only a few seconds before they went off. Almost immediately, the smoke permeated a twenty-square-foot area in the rear of the club where one of its three bars was. People began screaming and then running for their lives. Junga had a hold on Tasha before they were both grabbed out front.

That's when the 50 caliber rifles started in on punching softball-size holes into the front wall above the front doors of the racy luxurious establishment. Out back, the MK-18 "street sweeper" opened up as well at every car it could take apart. It only took about a minute and a half for a thousand clubgoers to come pouring out onto the street. No one had expected what were later called *weapons of war* to be used at the beloved nightclub.

Joker got Natasha out of there. As they spun up out of there - tires screeching like crazy - Joker was able to lock eyes with Vinnie as he turned the corner and disappeared. Joker gritted his teeth, wanting to go back and kill him, but he didn't because he didn't have all the facts.

The first thing Joker did was take Tasha's cell phone and throw it out of the moving Sprinter that he drove out to East New York where the 18-wheeler was parked at. Most of the crew were shut up inside of the trailer and driven upstate once everyone was accounted for.

"What about the wife and the son?" Tasha asked.

"They were given a stolen car, and they are likely on their way back to Brooklyn."

"So I got played I guess… this is where you gon' say '*told ya so?*'" Natasha stated emotionless.

"You put us all in danger for what? Cuz you wanna fuck and suck?" Joker inquired slowly.

"Well, I'm grown," she said defiantly.

"Don't be proud," he cautioned. "You put my crew in danger. You see how they ride? They ride cuz we family. You put us in danger again, you can take ya grown ass on. You just started another war."

She bit her tongue because she knew she had done something she shouldn't have. They pulled up at an Airbnb fully furnished ranch-style home in Nanuet. One with a 2.2 million price tag. The 18-wheeler parked and faint barking was heard in the distance.

"C'mon, we got a place to lay up, eat, and sleep," Joker mumbled before he looked at his sister and hugged her. "Next time you want someone to take them panties off, talk to ya bro. Don't we fuckin' talk?"

Natasha stared at him. "Why you have fantasies of havin' me in private? Your *sister*?" she sneered.

Ariel's ears perked up at hearing incest between siblings. *Again.* Iani and Uzenna were two mad hot black sisters, and it was like they were making "*Incest Marathon Video XXX*" or something the way they did it. Ariel had seen them. Iani and Uzenna were on the sofa, naked, in front of the fire, Iani had Uzenna pinned, her legs bent back with Iani's left knee up by Uzenna's right breast, and she sat her bald wet cunt down on top of Uzenna's and them two ladies *went in*. They lost their minds in the sounds, the squishy, smacking, wet noises, the smells of raw creamy light brown pussies lighting up the air like fried chicken wings or something.

"Yeah...right. *Hell no,* freaky-leeky," Joker said, laughing with her. "I mean there's male strip clubs. You can own as many of them sorry bastards as you want now. Matter of fact," Joker whispered, "Lieutenant Gates? I thought he'd make a great husband for you."

"He is...he *will* but I got that blood you got, bro," Natasha admitted. "It's like I get up in the middle of the night hot as fuck."

"Don't marry my dude then. Do you but be goddamn safe doin' it," Joker advised. "Stay under my protection cuz this shit is real."

She hugged him and went inside the two-story ten-bedroom house with everyone else. Only Bible and Bushwacker found Joker in the mansion's home office. He called Don Braga straight off the rip. Joker looked at his men.

"The Mafia tryna get us hit," Joker said. "Why else would Vinnie pop up in New York right now?"

____

CHAPTER 14

____

You Don't Understand War
<u>West Palm Beach, FL</u>

JOKER, Ariel, Apolina, Satzi, Boo, and Bible flew back down to Florida to regroup. This was going to be a gigantic move he was thinking about so he needed all hands on deck. A flawless plan had to be devised, and it would take some time. The Bragas were acting funny when Joker already told them that Ghostman was dead over what he did to Vinnie's mistress, Jessika Cicero, among his other betrayals.

On top of that, Joker knew that Folk was Ghostman's peoples so there was that. The Golden Lions were too formidable an enemy to not go to war with them. Especially after Folk had already taken the first shot by snatching up his sister.

Folk's wife and son were dead. Killed by Young Army and their bodies were cremated at an upstate horse crematorium. Joker had given the order and subsequently admitted it to Natasha.

"You don't understand war, big sis," he told her. "But I lied so you wouldn't make a scene up in New York."

"That was still some cold shit," she accused him.

"I agree but I ain't out here playin' games wit these niggas who

95

tryna kill us," Joker barked. "Enjoy da fuckin' luxury I bled for and my team bled for. You can have any mansion, any house car, wardrobe whatever now…enjoy it."

They were at the spectacular 28,893 square foot Mediterranean style super villa with a hefty $18.5 million dollar price tag in West Palm Beach, Florida. They had only been staying there temporarily until their individual luxury homes were built in the exclusive gated community. There was a total of ten beautiful homes built and each was in the $2 million dollar range. Today was moving day.

They left the West Palm Beach mansion for their own homes just a few miles away. Uzenna and their three-year-old son, David Leon, had the house on the very end of the Cul de Sac. It had a sandy cliff that led down to the mile of beach they owned. Coral and their three-year-old son, Bradford, went inside of their own house. Ashley and their three-year-old daughter, Sonja, entered their own house. It was the same with the others: Leah and David II, Eden and Eve, Valerie and Ivory Brown Hodges, Iani and little Rose, Brittani, and David III, and of course, even though King Mendo Hodges' mother was dead, he stayed with Uzenna and David Leon Junior. That was nine houses.

Joker looked at Boo and Satzi. "There's other houses being built on the land. This tenth one is for the EIE security and y'all's families. Some of E.I.E. have their own houses already, which is cool. So y'all figure it out. We'll get some trailers installed up here if we got to. Lemme know. Security gotta be cut rate."

Later in the evening, Joker left Uzenna at home where she was ordering food via Instacart. He only had Ariel along for the ride. They had to go to Home Depot to order some household items. They pulled into the parking lot of a strip mall area where the Home Depot was. Ariel was laughing and giggling inside the store, happy to be alone with the man she had a crush on.

"I heard you were partyin' wit Young Army shorty," he chided her.

"Huh?" she asked, flabbergasted.

"Huh nuttin'," he said, playfully elbowing her.

Two men came from the front and two more from the rear. It was more sudden than the changing wind. Gunshots rang out. Joker was equipped with double Glocks with automatic switches and extended clips. Ariel was struck in the back and the head and crumpled to the floor like a pair of stockings. Joker had on a bulletproof hoodie, but he was still hit in the throat!

His double Glocks ripped and punched holes wildly at everything else but the shooters at first. *GREASEHEADS*, he thought. *Hitters*! But he ended up taking them all out anyway while severely wounded! Screaming could be heard as shoppers ran for their lives.

When it was over Joker looked at Ariel and she was dead, eyes wide open. He bent down with blood dripping out of his neck. He took off his shirt and put pressure on the wound. He searched the men for identification but found none. *Professionals,* he thought. *That's a fact.* Then he exited the store, made it out to the bulletproof Denali, and pulled off. He made it all the way home where he crashed into the mailboxes on the corner and a short brick wall not far away.

In the distance, he heard Uzenna screaming. That's when Joker Red felt the light of the world turn more darker than he'd ever seen it.

"No, no, Daddy… Daddy, no!" Uzenna screamed as she opened the door and saw him slumped over to the right. "Call the ambulance!"

The ambulance came but hours passed when the large army of Joker's friends and family were informed that he was in a coma…and doctors were worried that he might not make it.

Part Three

THE COMA, THE DREAMS

He was obsessed with the beautiful Bronx, New York Hip Hopper Ice Spice. She sweats sex appeal. As he stared at the deep groove of Heather Sampson's ass he fantasized that it was a naked ICE SPICE on his bed pulling those lovely yellow ass apart, displaying all of her honey-dripping goodies. He buried his nose into her juicy mango and swallowed every liquid sugary deposit. His favorite scent was her lemony-scented anal…Which he licked, and licked, and kept on licking…

-From Jokers Coma Dreamz

CHAPTER 15

Joker's Dreams of Ice Spice

"YOU CAN TELL me if you have a girlfriend," the cute corrections department nurse flirted with the Brooklyn bank robber and gang leader.

His eyes watched her prance past him in her pink pants, her ass jiggling just right like *Ice Spice*, the superstar rapper chick from the Bronx, New York where stars were born. There he was again…Joker was obsessed with Ice Spice who's set so far apart from any other female Hip Hopper - ever. That girl had a sweet sex appeal and she had one of the most infectious smiles he'd ever seen amongst any female on the earth – ever. She made people, particularly him, just wish so badly that he could hug her and be hugged back by her. Joker compared every chick he was attracted to to Ice Spice. He was staring at the groove that sliced Heather Sampson's ass and as he wondered if she had on anything beneath the pink scrub pants; he found himself trying to imagine what Ice Spice's ass looked like, bent over, totally naked. Then as her pretty hands reached back, grabbed the soft round halves, spread them wide-like two halves of a very large mango melon. And right there for him to see…to smell…the cute little asshole of Ice

Spice…The lovely vagina of Ice Spice and her warm, beautiful Goddess-like scent.

"Huhn? Goddess-like scent?" Heather Sampson grinned, her incredibly pretty eyes staring at him.

Joker snapped out of it. He must have been stuck thinking about the rapper with the pumpkin-colored hair. "Yeah, you smell like that J-Lo or Mariah perfume or somethin'," he lied, fronting like he was sweeping in case the officer came by to look.

"Thank you," she said.

"But girlfriend? Nah. Friends, that's girls? Yeah," he admitted.

"Didn't think you did," the dark chocolate-skinned, 150-pound nurse mentioned. As she put away some papers inside of a file cabinet Joker couldn't take his eyes off of her curvaceous 5 foot 5 inch frame. "I can tell you're a man's man, you're light-skinned, green eyes… pretty hair…You drive the women crazy, don'tchu?"

He shrugged, his eyes searching for that bitch ass Spanish C.O. Garcia. They usually took their eyes off Joker Red because he worked alone and there were other male nurses in the area. They were all in different offices. Joker knew when the best time was to holler at the newer, younger nurses. That time was now.

The newer nurses dug the shit out of Joker. They knew he was somebody on the street. And he was also one of those New York prisoners sent to James T. Vaughn Correctional Center in Smyyna, Delaware. A spot nobody ever heard of. Some Corrections Sergeant named Stephen Floyd was kidnapped and held hostage in the 2017 "*C-Building Riot*." They tried to frame it in the *USA Today* – owned News Journal, DelawareOnline.com/JamesTVaughnCorrectionalCenter, that the whole prison rioted when it was only two dozen. Fake motherfuckin' news. They held Sergeant Floyd and a few other C.O.s/staff hostage, Joker was informed.

Sergeant Stephen Floyd, of course, had called for backup but all of those years of being a bitch ass punk bastard had finally caught up with him. The COs, other sergeants, lieutenants, and captains that he cried over the radio to help him abandoned him like that bitch cop did in Uvalde, Texas. However, that elementary school cop was being expected to run into a hail of fucking .223 and Hydrashock rounds. The men who abandoned Floyd's dumb ass had pepper spray billy clubs and such against inmates with their fists. Karma's a bitch. Floyd got what he was giving out to other inmates.

"Fuck Floyd" was what Joker heard. That sonofabitch beat up other inmates, lied on hundreds of write-ups; to spite inmates, he refused to let visitors in to see inmates and tried to screw as many inmates' wives and girlfriends as he could and then come back into the prison to admit it when he was successful. At the end of the riot, Stephen Floyd was located with his genitals removed, stuffed in his mouth, and a broomstick shoved up his ass. One inmate said it best: "It ain't no fun when the rabbit gets the gun." Then to add insult to the Delaware DOC's ego injury the prosecutor tried about 20 inmates. There was only one person who was found guilty, and all the other charges were dismissed. The so-called hardest cat out of everybody – Royal Downs from Maryland – snitched on everybody involved. He had life but now he's free.

"What are you thinkin' about?" HBS, Heather Beatrice Sampson, jarred Joker Red back to reality.

He shook his head. "You asked if I had a girlfriend. Do you have a boyfriend? My turn to question you."

"A husband," she told him as he held a broom to act like he was sweeping. The C.O. on duty sometimes looked back to see if Joker was working.

He was checking her out. "Cheat on him," Joker told her as he made his way past her and into the maintenance closet where supplies were kept.

"No!" she said, watching him as he pulled out the longest, thickest light brown dick she'd ever seen. Sooner or later she knew that it was going to happen. Each day she came to work and saw him, they quietly flirted.

"You thought I was fuckin' jokin'?" he asked as he slowly stroked his hardening shaft. "You thought I was lyin' when I said I got a porno king cock. Ain't no lyin' on Joker Red, bitch. Now get yo sweet dark chocolate ass over here," he urged her, showing her his scrotum, which reminded her of a great big orange. "Come and kiss it."

The cute dark-skinned nurse, who Joker called his *"dime-minus two,"* saw the C.O. twenty yards up the corridor having a loud animated discussion about the New York Football Giants devastating loss to the Dallas Cowboys the evening before.

"The Giants, Knicks, and Yankees owners have no interest in winning championships! As long as they have their mansions, Maybach's, Rolexes, and nineteen-year-old mistresses, they don't give a fuck. When New York sports fans stop going to those funeral of a game they put on and stop buying their loser-stamped merchandise maybe the owners will start caring!"

She put on her white lab coat and stepped into the maintenance closet. "Kiss you?" she asked, reaching out to touch him. "It's so big! The heads are big like a… like a brown egg! I can't put that thing in my mouth… it's too small."

But she already made up her mind. She grabbed him with both hands and he put an arm around her tiny waist, pulling her closer. He bent to kiss Meagan Goode's lips which were moist with her great-tasting saliva. It had been 8 months since his last piece of ass and he aimed to enjoy his little chocolate shortcakes. This one he wanted *all* of her holes. Chicks like her, with the nicest asses, were advertising what they had back there like a mufucka, even if they had never been butt-fucked.

Joker Red was a pretty light-skinned nigga with green eyes, and wavy, well-trimmed hair. He was above average height-wise so to women, he was always taller. He was not only a boxer, but he excelled at martial arts, and as an Army Ranger, he did well in close-quarter/military combat; with a knife, he was an opponent's worst nightmare. He was a killer, didn't mind killing, he even liked it – some. Needless to say, his body was rock solid. Unbelievably rock-hard and jacked body of the gods and not the huge Mr. Olympia type either.

"Touch here, too, dollface," he whispered, lifting his shirt to show her his torso. Eight-pack. Pectorals on point. Hard M-A-N 100%.

"Oh my God." She kissed his chest and belly, taking in his scent. Her lawyer husband was soft, out of shape, and fat.

She sat down on the milk crate with the blanket folded and

placed on top of it. She had him wait a quick second so she could check on the whereabouts of the C.O. He was still in the same spot. She was nervous. If she were caught she'd be arrested but the thrill of fucking an inmate had her pussy all sticky and creamy inside of her panties.

Before she sat back down her was on her again. With both hands full of her phat and super soft ass. Reminded him of this C.O. bitch named Miss Watson who let him grab her ass when she realized that he wasn't from there, that he was a different breed. The C.O. there had photos circulating of him and a few rogue Rangers torching millions of dollars of Taliban heroin money – so that the Army Generals couldn't get it. And the Homeland…and the CIA. Especially them. As word went that was the real reason why Joker Red and his EIE crew were discharged.

Miss Watson was floored when Joker Red dropped his towel on her one day in his cell. He'd been grooming himself as he always did and there C.O. Watson was. She saw that meat and thought she'd been seeing things. Joker wasn't into measuring nothing except the days he had left in prison. She saw a foot long, 12 inches. And almost every day after that she'd find a way to suck Joker's giant juicy dick and swallow his hot streams of sticky cum. Whenever she was done her lips would get swollen and her clit hard but she'd scurry off to the bathroom to finger fuck her hand. Other times Joker would put her on her knees and eat her wet pussy from behind so she could get her nut off which she did. But for the most part she just wanted him to grab her ass and let her grab his cock through his pants because she was so nervous.

But fuck that bitch.

Heather Beatrice Sampson's turn. She looked up at him as she gently took hold of his huge balls with one hand. Sweat was breaking out like little itty-bitty tiny stars in the night on her forehead. "It's so big," she kept saying in her small voice as her left hand encircled the brown egg-sized dick head. "God your cock is so big. I don't think-" she kissed and licked the head. "-it'll fit -" opening wider than ever, "-in my mouf -!" she gagged and coughed.

"There…oohhh, fuck yeah, Heather, suck my dick, baby," he urged her on. "Mmm, that feels good!"

He sat on the ledge of the white industrial sink and kept a lookout down the hall. He told the lovely nurse that all was well. She made the prettiest dick-sucking songs imaginable. Reminded Joker Red of certain records found on *iHeartRadio* that many niggas listened to while masturbating in the privacy of their cells late at night: *Sexy Licking Noises; ASMR Lesbians Making Love; Fuck Pussy; Swell Audio; Sex & Beats; Gina79*, etcetera. If niggas wanted to make money off of downloads sex sells but DOC had been blocking the obvious ones. The hustle cats had to make their sex noise tracks look normal and put an ad in KITE magazine so niggas could catch it. And real hustle bitches who want to supplement their income needed to get in the circle with book writers from urbanaintdead.com because them cats were out to make money - they're waiting for that real ride or die to come along.

Joker Red could see how Heather was getting all into it now. Her lips were stretched, and she was taking half of that juicy dark tan bone into her throat while her two fists stroked the balls and his remaining dick up and down, making Joker proud and putting him on the verge of bussing his thick hot semen all into her face. But he wanted to make sure all the months of his backed-up sperm were shot into her belly via that little hole between her legs.

He pulled his dick away from her and she immediately thought the worst. "It's okay, pretty young thing."

He looked down the hall. The cop was once again seated at his desk, looking like he was about to go to sleep. Perfect timing.

"You like how it tastes?" Joker asked her.

"I love how it tastes," she told him. He held her and put his warm hands into her panties, one in the front and the other in the back. She poked her ass at his fingers and he found that she was soaking wet from how horny sucking his dick made her. "I know I'm wet…I came like four times. All I have to do is rub my clit against where I'm sitting and cum."

He pulled her scrubs down and ripped the panties clean off of her.

"Well…I…what if we did it next time?" she asked as he held her damp black satin panties up to his nose, made sure he exhaled all the way, closed his mouth, and inhaled through his nose, smelling her pungent cunt scent. His dick was rubbing her pussy lips unintentionally and she grabbed the Monster and rubbed her clitoris, smashed up against it. "You gon' be the life and the death of me," she whined.

"Why you wanna wait til next time?" he questioned.

"All that vaginal moisture, the orgasms…it smells strong," she said like a mouse, in that small cute voice of hers. "Don't it?"

Joker kissed her on those soft lips. He French-kissed her warm, sweet pretty mouth. "I can kiss you all day… when I come home, you gon' be my wifey, ain't you?"

"What about…? Fuck him. Fuck my husband. Hell yeah, Joker Red."

Joker bent on his knees and kissed that beautiful black ass, loving this hot dark-skinned young nurse. He told her, "Buss them cheeks open all the way…open 'em!"

He sniffed her and licked a hot wet trail down that dark black crack, accentuated by the pink insides of her wet glistening pussy and the dark purplish inner labia minora as she opened it *way* open like the front doors of a candy shop. The clit poked out.

"It all smells good to me, ya hear me, Heather baby?" He breathed in her left ear, rubbing that great big dick into her little pink hole.

She nodded. "Yes…It all smells good, Joker Red…I love placing my fingers down there and tasting and smelling my privates. I'm not gay but I think about women and how their cunts smell. I can cum while masturbating and smelling my pussy and my ass. I smell so good, huhn?" Her insecurities had disappeared.

"You do. A strong scent isn't the wrong scent," he frenched her like she just married him. "You a pretty bitch. All of you is bad as fuck. Damn, I wish I had a wife like you – you woulda been pregnant already cuz my dick plants the seed right on the egg." He fingered her pussy, slowly making it leak."

"I'm so ready…show me, Big Daddy."

CHAPTER 16

<u>"Joker Sleeps"</u>

JOKER RED LOOKED out one more time and he saw that the fat C.O. was asleep.

"Imma fuck you now okay?" But he was already two inches inside of that special dark chocolate, hurting her tight little sugar pack, but all that hurt shot straight to her clit, nipples, and anus.

"Fuck me. My husband only does it when I'm ovulating," she let slip out, but what Joker was doing had the little nurse a bit delirious.

It took several minutes for Joker to sink the entire missile inside of her. First, he was fucking her like a male horse did a mare, just slamming that incredibly long, thick, dark tan cucumber in and out of her.

"OHHHHH, SHHHHH! FUUUUCCCCCKKKKK!" Joker had her on the floor in missionary with her cumming all over his gigantic cock. He was slicing in and out, hammering her. "Should I pull out?!" he asked. "Or can I cum inside you?"

"I want your cum, Big Daddy," she begged as the earth shook beneath her wild orgasm. "Aaoww! Aaow!"

"SHH!" he told her as his nut busted inside of her. "Look down there, Mama. How can dat tiny pussy take all that dick?"

There was so much of his cum that spurted inside of her that it drained out over her perineum and down over her even smaller hairless asshole which looked like a star emoji or maybe an asterisk. Whatever it was he knew she wanted to be fucked there.

He made her get dressed and get out of there. No time for cuddling. He grabbed a broom and started sweeping. "Hey, Dark Chocolate…"

She sat in front of a fan, trying to cool off. "Huhn?"

"You gon' feel me runnin' outta your hot little pussy and down your leg for the rest of the day. Don't wash up so you can smell me 'til you get in the shower tonight."

She grinned as he walked away. To herself: *My God! I'm ovulating and we had no condom*, she was thinking. Little Chocolate Heather had always walked a straight line. She worked harder than all the White girls in her classes at Syracuse University. Those uppity fucking Asian bitches, too – meaning South Korean, Vietnamese, and especially the Indian girls who need to look in the goddamned mirror sometimes and see that they're also Black.

Heather was beautiful but didn't fully understand her beauty enough to embrace it. *Fuck it. It didn't matter now,* she thought as she made her rounds through the prison infirmary. After she did all of her area checks she returned to the office area. She was ready to go home.

Joker had mopped the corridor and went from office to office picking up all the trash from small trashcans and he emptied them into the larger one on the cart he pushed around.

"Chocolate Heather," he said as she sat at her desk. "Whatchu thinkin'?"

She turned in her swivel office chair. "That was the wildest thing I've ever done. I married the first man I was with…and we've been trying to get pregnant. This morning, I found out that I was ovulating and didn't tell him because the attraction was gone."

"Well I won't be in here forever," Joker told her. "And I'm no bum."

She nodded and slit her eyes. "We heard about you, Mr. Hodges."

His government name was David Hodges.

Joker Red had a million-dollar smile that melted women with one gold tooth laced with a sparkling diamond in it which lit up his entire yellow face. *"We heard?"* he repeated. He liked shorty.

"Yeah. You bein' an Army Ranger, a hero with a death wish?" she said it in a question form.

"You ever go to Wikipedia for anything?" he asked.

"Everyone does," she told him.

He nodded for a second. "Yeah. But I can go on there right now, create a page for you, and tell every White American racist fuckin' lie in existence aboutchu. I can make it look beautiful? Flawless. They run a background check on you your reputation's destroyed. The point: don't believe the hype."

She giggled. "What about all the videos online of you as Sergeant Hodges: Bur Baby Burn? You burned millions and millions of dollars when you were ordered to return it to your commander. That was the coolest thing I've ever seen. You could've taken it, hid it."

"I flew over villages in Kandahar givin' away even more than that," Joker stated, waving his hand as two more nurses came into the room. A White/Latina chick with brown hair, slender, average height for a woman, and her name was Alicia Silas. "Hello, nurses."

"Hi, Red," Miss Silas greeted him.

"Wassup," the other nurse was Imani Henry. 30 years old, shorty had long beautiful black hair like one of those extremely poor Bangladeshi girls but whenever they were in a TV commercial or on BBC News, their young women were among the prettiest in the world. Joker told Imani, "I swear, Bangladesh is broker than a mutha but them young ladies' hair is so beautiful. Your hair Imani…JEE-ZUS CHRIST! Ya hear me?"

Silas was snapping her fingers and laughing along with Heather. "Earth to David Joker Red Hodges! Come back down!"

Imani grabbed her hair and told Joker, "Thank you, Mr. Hodges, for being nice to me today. I've already thought the same thing when I see Bangladeshi hair. Great compliment. Got any more?"

"Of course but things like that need to come organically, ya diggin' what I'm tellin' you?" he told Imani Henry who was the same height as Chocolate Heather. Imani did have the look of some exotic mixture, but she was just so fine that God gave this little bitch something extra. She had a caramel and brown sugar complexion like the color of the sand in the Sinai Desert of Egypt.

Joker Red called Chocolate Heather his "dime minus two" but Imani and Silas were both "dimes minus one point five." In Red's book, that's a substantial jump.

Heather looked like she was ready to go. She knew she had to get home to shower and douche before her husband got home and caught sight and scent of another man's cum running out of her. On top of that, he knew that she was ovulating – she'd texted him earlier – so he would be raring to go.

The officer's shift changes in New York State prisons are 7 AM – 3 PM; 3 PM – 11 PM; and 11 PM – 7 AM, same for the nurses, no ifs, ands, or buts. There wasn't a damned thing to do in the Block after 3PM for Joker except to hit the 300–man shower house. That's where inmates showered, did business, socialized, smoked cigarettes, and weed, and headed back into the Block.

Joker had money stashed but he was a mysterious cat so no one knew how much. He didn't run his mouth. Because of his reputation, his cool-ass swag, and superior I.Q., he was given room to breathe.

He was inside the Medical Building from 7 AM to 11 PM except for when he wished to shower or do something else. After showering he came back to work just as the evening nurse staff returned from passing out "PM Medication."

"Mr. Hodges?" Nurse Silas called out to him. "One second please?"

He got up from where he was sitting reading the New York Post and came to her office in the back of the larger *Nurse's Station.* "Yeah, Miss Silas? Vanilla Silas?"

She smirked sarcastically. "Why do you call me that?"

"Cuz…" he shrugged.

"Becuz I'm White…*ish*? I'm Polynesian-British and Hawaiian," she informed him. "I heard you were a genius. *Polynesia.*"

Joker had a signature disarming smile for the bitches. "Too easy, Vanilla Silas. Oceania. Bunch of islands in central, South Pacific. Sort of between New Zealand, and Easter Island. Some Polynesian women I've been around are the most beautiful on the planet. You have the blood of Gods and Goddesses inside of you."

She was impressed. "Can you get here at 6 AM?"

"Tomorrow?"

She nodded. "To wax the floor."

"Yeah, you have to write a pass and I'll drop it off to my building clerk to be signed. You be here that early?"

"When I'm behind on paperwork. Yeah."

"Vanilla, the plant," he told her, then walked away.

"But what's it got to do with m-" but he was out of ear range. She spoke to herself, "What's that got to do with callin' me that?"

CHAPTER 17

**The Scent of Vanilla
<u>In Deep Sleep</u>**

JOKER WAS ALREADY DONE LAYING down his third coat of wax when "Vanilla" Silas arrived. She'd asked him to be there by 6 AM but he'd left with the first wave of inmate *"Cadre Workers"* at 4:45 AM. Those were the cats who worked making sewer caps insides of the "Foundry"; others were off to the automotive shop where they fixed cars that belonged to the state workers/agencies. There were other jobs like those where inmates were paid $280 per month to start but there were others – like a homie of Joker's named Bama aka Blue Boy from Williamsburg in Brooklyn, who came to prison with a six-year sentence, but now had life. Blue Boy was a young "pretty boy" Puerto Rican that a lot of people had love for out B-K. He came to prison and them so-called tough guys thought they could beat on Blue and steal what little he had. Blue Boy boiled some hot water with sugar and lemon juice in it. Then he waited until the perfect moment approached and he dumped it into one of the dude's face, neck, and chest. While he screamed, was blinded, and skin peeled, Blue Boy aired his ass out, crashing the dude's face in with his fists and then the bottom heel of his black Timberland chukkas, killing him. Blue Boy got 25 years for that body. Then he stabbed the shit out of a C.O., hurting him so bad that he could never talk again. Then Blue Boy killed two more inmates until he had 95 years to life. Now he was so legendary that nobody even blinked at him wrong.

Joker bumped into Blue Boy that morning and received an envelope from him. After they spoke Joker headed on over to work and laid out three thin coats of wax already.

"How long you been here?" Silas asked Joker as she stood in front of all the yellow "WET FLOOR" caution cones that he had set up.

"'Bout 4:55 AM," he told her. "It's dry… come on."

The officer did a quick round. All he wanted to do was go back to sleep anyhow.

"How long does it take for a coat of that stuff to dry?" the sexy exotic, Polynesian British mixed, honey-sweet nurse inquired.

Joker looked at her. "If you put a thin layer of that succulent Fenty lip gloss on those yummy pink lips it'll last only a little while, right?"

"That's an inappropriate way to speak to me but…yeah, you're correct," she said, turning to open up her office. She was wearing burgundy scrubs, but he could still see the curves of that jiggly ass. And being a jail nigga deprived of a woman for a while, all he did every day was analyze the bodies of bitches. Where there was ass there was sphincter, even the perineum on a girl became a thing of beauty – where a man wanted to plant his face, nose, chin, and cheekbones. It all smelled good and tasted like good-ass BBQ ribs or some shit. Joker was no different. Never before did he want a chick's ass so bad either. And not only the booty cheeks or the bootyhole but – as long as it was clean – his tongue wanted *in*. Every inch of the curve of the crack, he wanted to kiss and make that coochie as hot as it could get, then start in on that pretty little thing. She cleared her throat. "Joker Red, my garbage can is filled up," she said.

"Oh, aight." He got up and came inside the small office. "Oh, yup," he quipped.

She'd pulled down her scrub pants with her back turned to him.

"All the girls know that you're a perfect lovemaker and Heather told us you had an eleven-inch monster. Is that true?"

His huge cock was hard in an instant. "Yeah…you wanna see it?" He was grabbing his dick, staring at her lovely asscheeks. She had some dude's name tattooed on the left cheek.

"You better go put a thick coat of wax on the floor out there, so it acts as an early warning alarm for us," she advised him. He was trying to see if he could get a glance of her watery wet pussy lips from the angle he was standing at but he could not.

He spun around, grabbed the mop, and laid out a very thick coat of wax on the off-white linoleum tile floor. Then he reentered the nurse's station. He stepped inside the small office, locked the door, and watched as Miss Silas removed her scrub v-neck shirt. Joker got an eyeful. She was now completely nude, from her head to her super pretty white bare feet. Joker Red was a kid in a candy store, and he told her that. Even as he said so he could tell that she was still a little nervous.

He showed her a stack of cash. "Don't worry 'bout the officer. Imma very powerful man, okay? He's one of ours."

Joker saw her nod and relax, saying to him, "Okay."

"Look at all this candy." He lifted her and sat her on top of her desk. She had rosé wine-colored nipples on what he guessed were 32D cup breasts which were perfect for a babe her size and weight. "Don't think I even seen a more gorgeous or more firm pair of thirty-two Dees that stood up."

"Suck them and bite my nipples real hard!" she begged as lust laced in her voice. "Put me on the red carpet. On the floor. I just have to try to suck your giant cock."

But he was already sucking her sexy titties. They were so pretty that he was close to bussing and splashing thick semen all over her belly, pussy, and thighs. He grabbed both of her wrists and pinned them way over her head so he could lick and slather his tongue all around her big knockers and he licked her smoothly-shaven underarms. She never had a man so wildly into her that he licked her and smelled her there. She caught him staring down at her and it was right there inside of that moment that she became 1000% his possession. He entered the wet and juicy slice of heaven between her legs for just a long…deep… breathtaking…moment but no way it could fit when the nigga she was dealing with was barely six inches.

"Oooohhh, it caaaannn!" she cried. She wanted that big monster cock so bad but he took it from her.

"Uh uh. I ain't hurtin' this sweet ass pussy. C'mere," he commanded her. He laid out on his back and she knew what to do. But first, she wanted affection. She laid down on top of him and they lovingly French-kissed. "Um, damn I love fuckin' kissin' you. Youse a badass bitch. Sit on my face and … don't try to take it all. Jus lick it mommie. Lick that sweet brown cucumber."

She sat on his face, twirling her yummy dripping sweets up and down his face with her soft brown pussy hair. The hairs on her cunt helped smear her musky female juices from his forehead to his chin. He loved looking up inside of her pink-hot pink pussy and her asshole He opened her up and had his fill.

As she gyrated her anus into his nose his tongue ate up all of her creamy juices. Meanwhile, she licked the gigantic cock from tip to base and she was able to deepthroat 7-8 inches of him. Silas knew how to sword-swallow a dick, jerk it, spit on it, and do all the nasty things he liked.

He put her back underneath him and re-entered her hot buttery tight cunt. This time she was more than ready.

"Heather was right. My God, she was right!" Miss Silas declared in her sweetest whimper and grind. "You have a whole foot of thick, long cock and you know how to fuck so good! Fuck me, Red. Fuck my tight Polynesian-British pussy!"

"Hell yeah, damn! Talk dat nasty shit. You know why I call you Vanilla now, right? Huh, you pretty big titty little slut? You understand it now, right?" he demanded an answer. ***Shclip! Smack! Shclip! Slap! Smack!*** The sex sounds made.

She saw him getting as sweaty as she was and the sexy "*shclip*" and "*smack*" sounds got more and more pronounced the sweatier they became and the wetter her cunt juices flowed to mix with his pre-ejaculate, and he sure had plenty. He could get a chick pregnant with the pre-cum alone.

"No," she whimpered as she experienced another mini-orgasm from feeling her clitoris react wildly against his grinding stir and also feeling his humongous balls tapping her anus.

He reached underneath and soaked in four fingers in the sensual sea salty sex cream. Propping himself up on his left elbow he cupped the back of her head and as he tongue kissed the slender beauty, he spread her juices on her upper lip, his upper lip, and shared the job of licking all of it off and smelling it.

"Smells?" he asked while slowly making love to her.

"Vanilla," she answered. And it turned something on inside of her because she grabbed his back and ass, throwing her little pussy hard up at him, fucking him as good as he was fucking her.

"You gon' always be my little vanilla slut, ain't you?"

"I wanna be your slut. Fuck my slutty pussy! Harder! Keep fuckin' me." She bit his ear and neck. "Fuck me hard. Fuck… I keep cummin' on this big black Mandingo dick. You love white girls, huh? You crazy 'bout white milky skin and flower pink pussy, right?"

He nodded, perspiration dropping all over her as he laid into that pretty pink-lipped bitch. "Fuck yeah. I want babies witta bad white slut bitch like you."

Her cunt went crazy with contractions and an orgasm ripped through her that seemed to crack something inside of her neck.

Joker had to kiss her to keep her quiet and the way she fucked him back made his nut blow and off went like five huge leaps of his dick, spurting out five ball-emptying blasts of semen into Vanilla Silas' gyrating pussy. He filled her vagina with his wet gushing man juices.

He rubbed his face all in between her big tits and kissed her more lovingly than she'd ever been kissed before. "Damn, damn, damn! I haveta get home. I want you so bad you just don't know," he moaned.

"I do know. I do," she assured him. "I'll be here for you. Me and Heather and Imani will," she said in a promising tone. "Of course-*discreetly*."

"I wanna talk to y'all," he stated. "On a cell."

They got dressed. "Okay…I can get it."

He handed her $1000. "Look, I need a iPhone, USB charger, and when you get it, put it in the bottom of your trashcan. Each time I get a phone you'll get $500. I can sell any good $150 phone for $500. But an iPhone is top dollar."

She was with it. She put the money away, kissed him, and they parted ways moments later.

CHAPTER 18

<u>Still In A Coma</u>

IN NEW YORK STATE the convicts (or inmates – as Delaware cats called themselves) were used to living a way that Delaware niggas couldn't even fathom. There was no way in hell that Joker would even bend over and be less than a man like these people tried to force him to be.

"No way in da fuck, homie," he muttered to himself as he trimmed his mustache and 5 o'clock shadow inside of his cell. James T. Vaughn Correctional Center was one of those pro-gay prisons that housed two grown men – with all their "property" or belongings – inside the same cell. A cell that was originally designed for one man. But the modern-day slave masters (the prison owners, the fucking governors, politicians, etc.) got greedy and in lieu of expanding the prisons for more bed space they simply installed bunk beds. "Wack ass shit…"

Blue Boy walked by Joker's open cell door. "You talkin' to yo'self, duke?" the Puerto Rican killer asked him.

"Always," Joker told him as he brushed the stray hairs off his neck and chest. He looked at his watch. "Ayo Blue, you be sure to meet me wit two stacks same time tomorrow mornin'."

Blue flashed four gold teeth on the bottom when he smiled. "Finally, niggaroni? The mouse you mean?"

"Fuck you mean *finally*?" Joker said in a low voice even though he had no "celly" (or cellmate). Still, the walls had ears. There was a big vent inside of each cell that cons used to communicate through. Every prison was different like in New York for instance. The prisoners up there drained all the water out of the toilet upstairs and the cell underneath him did the same. Afterward, the two cells were able to fish contraband back and forth between them. "And what da fuck's a niggaroni?"

Blue Boy, who had dark hair and was Joker Red's age – they were both 30 – shrugged. "I don't fuckin' know. But I mean we have been needing a mouse plug." ("Mouse" meaning cellphone)

Joker Red pulled the door to his cell shut and nodded. "Yeah, I know. They all slowed down, Delaware. Not like stupid low IQ slow but stuck back in the 1950's. It's normal here not to make money…not have phones and be broke."

The day before, Joker had been given his first cellphone by Vanilla Silas. A move which had mildly surprised him because out of the micro-circle of nurses that he was fucking, Vanilla Silas seemed the most nervous out of three. He gave Blue Boy the phone because that was his man. Blue Boy was a Latin King "First Crown," (e.g., The King, or Boss).

"Oh shit, kid, this a *iPhone 15 Titanium*!" Blue stated, happy now, handshake hugging Joker.

"Aight, look…" Joker showed him how to get in and out of it.

"Here." Blue gave him a wadded-up envelope full of cash.

"That phone is mine and its more than a stack," Joker made it clear. "The mice I got comin' in are all gonna be iPhones but the older ones being resold by *HSN, QVC*, online spots like that."

"H-S-N like home shoppin' channel them old ladies watch all day?"

"*Home Shopping Network* is one of 'em, yeah." Joker nodded as Blue peeked out again. "If you want that same one I gotchu for two stacks."

Blue nodded. "Damn, you hittin' me hard, too."

"Son, we gotta keep the mules in Prada and LV or whateva else them bitches want," Joker said. "As for everyone else, I want six hondo each phone but charge 'em eight even so two hundred go yo way, cuz."

"Bet. Lemme hit *mi jefa* (my shorty) to ready that two stizzies for the phone," Blue said, making a call to his wifey real quick.

"I said tomorrow," Joker said, looking out his mans.

"I know you mad well, big homie. And knowing you, you already got da phone. You just on yo funny ass pretty boy throw-off-da-scent type deal," Blue stated right at the second his babe picked up.

Joker had the poker face on but Blue's ass was right. Joker had the phone.

"Same cash app?" Blue Boy inquired.

Joker shook his head. "Nah use this – but I always change up. Glad you asked. It's: *$IGHOSTWRITEBOOKS523@gmail.com.*"

"Sound like a email," Blue commented.

"It is. You know I write books but instead of just writin' for myself, I'm writing for others who feel like owning, marketing, and promoting a book or books," Joker explained once he was off the phone. "Pet project of mine. I'll explain more. I gotta be out, son."

Blue Boy took off. Joker was glad that he had it on his prison file to be housed alone. The New York State maximum security prisons did not house two men together in a cell with a bunk bed and a toilet in it. That was pro-gray shit. In Delaware, they housed two men together even in their supermax portion of the prison and created situations where men intentionally either got raped or were in danger of being raped. James T. Vaughn prison, for instance, would put a 250-pound 50-year-old, lifer, white racist, rapist in the room with a nineteen-year-old in prison for drug dealing and being a black drug addict. The DOC's motive? Well, what was their motive for letting Delaware's most dangerous serial rapist alone with a cute, young, white, female counselor who wore short tight skirts and had an ass like Cardi B's? Barack Miller, a big black motherfucker who had 600-plus years for raping all of them poor horrified females, saw, "that cute white bitch in that lil white dress and no panty lines!" Barack was heard telling other inmates, who were in the classrooms getting ready for school and group, was how Joker had heard the story of the July 2004 rape. Barack had been heard saying in front of some of the incompetent, bozo, asshole COs and other dickhead Delaware DOC idiots: *"Mmm... all I need is a few minutes with her the first time. It's the next time she better watch out for! Hahahaha!"* They even laughed with him.

But Barack wasn't joking. He knew he was never going home. Even cats with one life sentence had no incentive to behave well. Men could have life for a habitual drug possession sentence, attempted murder, or shooting a drug rival. And even after doing 20, 25, or more years with no violent acts it meant nothing. So once a man got it in his head to do something mad, the DOC said in the local news only that the state was justified in locking men up that long. Never would they take responsibility for driving a man mad. That went for prisoners everywhere. Barack was a serial killer. Nobody disputed that. Got along well with everybody. The counselor settled for a lofty amount of money and the DOC paid it to keep its secrets safe. Just like the State of Delaware made history when it paid out $7.55 million to Counselor Patricia May and others in that lawsuit following the 2017 inmate uprising in C-Building at James T. Vaughn Correctional Center.

"These mufuckaz pay out millions upon millions to keep the people who care from knowing the truth about their wicked ways and actions," Joker uttered to himself as he put the cash he'd made for the week into several tight rolls, put masking tape around them, then plastic wrap. He tucked the $5000 in drug money into the pocket part of his *Fruit of the Loom* brand "tightie-whities." He left his cell and locked it. "Sir Claus Moser wrote that *Education costs money but so does ignorance.*"

Joker knew that he was listed as a dangerous man. For that reason alone the DOC couldn't put another person in his cell. Not only had Sergeant Joker Red Hodges been trained by the United States Army Rangers, he was a battle-hardened killer. Guns, knives, missile systems, a tank...he loved killing with his own body the most and he understood that out of all the weapons a man could have, the mind was the most destructive thing he had. Being ignorant wasn't going to cost Joker a goddamn thing. New York thought they were fucking him around by moving them so far away. The first way they fucked up was that they sent him to a spot where the C.O.s were softer than a *Nick-elodeon* afternoon special. Another staff, in general, was uneducated – not completely dumb and stupid, just only when compared to him. The uneducated started on the bottom and so did their salaries.

This included the nurses, the psychological department, and the dental folks. The State of Delaware boasted the Presidential Family, the ritzy Greenville section of the State, and the multi-millionaire and billionaire Du Pont Family hierarch. The People and the State talked of all this money but the prison system's "services" were poor. Medical, Dental, Mental Health/Mental Health, and Drug Treatment. These services were premeditated and precalculated by the States political bigwigs to provide no drug treatment, no great long-term health care, and no meaningful aftercare/aka re-entry housing programs to *any* Delaware inmate specifically because the state desired an extremely high recidivism (return to prison) rate.

The DOC's main office in Dover, Delaware, had been signing off on $60 million, then $90 million-, and 98-million-dollar contracts to companies who provided medical/dental/and mental healthcare to prisons. Understanding the numbers game Joker Red saw immediately where to beam in on. He saw that the medical *"nurses"* for instance ain't even real hospital *Registered Nurses*, or RNs, as everyone knows them. They barely have any true blue RNs. The RNs command a way bigger salary than, say, a Medical Administrator or a Licensed Nurse Assistant *(LNA)*. Why have a real nurse when Centurion Correctional Services or Correctional Medical Services (aka "CMS") can hire four LNAs instead of the one RN's salary?

"Them hoez is broke," Joker noticed on his first day in prison. He almost laughed at them sorry ass bitches. They were cute…well, about fourteen percent were really at the top cute-wise. The others needed help. "I'm comin' at these bitches' wit hard dick and cash money."

The chips were falling just how he wanted them to.

CHAPTER 19

<u>**Dreams About Imani Henry**</u>

"Rehoboth? Where y'all live now?" he asked the sexy Polynesian-British-Hawaiian nurse who turned the 22-inch computer his way to show him an apartment she was checking out.

"I'm not far from the prison. I'm over -"

"Hold," Joker whispered as he started swinging the mop he held. Two mental health people, a white female, and a black male, approached Silas' office and entered. Joker went about his business cleaning up. He went into Heather Sampson's area and she was happy to see him.

"The laundry basket needs to go," she directed him.

He didn't hesitate. "Go inside of the ladies' bathroom, pull the trash liner out, and you'll see the rolls of cash. Go 'head, it's a lot so I'll wait."

She bee-lined to the bathroom and it took her a couple of minutes, but she came back out and nodded in his direction. He pushed the laundry cart down the corridor past the officer's desk where he had to stop so that the laundry could be checked.

"Keep it pushin', Hodges, wit da coronavirus laundry you handling back there," C.O. McCaulay said.

Joker went inside of the laundry basket room and removed the six cellphones and USB chargers. Once he had them he transported them directly back to his housing unit which was D-East. He put four of them into his locker, bolted it shut, and caught up with Blue Boy who was in his cell.

"You fuckin' back?" Blue was surprised. "Already?"

Joker hit him with two phones. "Move 'em. I gotta get back."

Blue was happy as a bird. "My mufucka."

Joker returned to work. He saw Vanilla seated behind her desk and Heather Sampson in chairs. "Y'all some boss chicks for real. Right to the point. I like it like that. No bullshittin'."

"Each of us brought them in through our food," Imani Henry said in a low voice when she walked into the office. "Five grand is a lot of money. Whattawe do wit-?"

"The phones, the happy meals, will mostly come in through those cash apps and the two Apple Pay accounts, okay?" he reiterated the cash routes. "Those phones and online payments accounts ain't attached to y'all. The iPhone 15 allows me to move the cash to my offshore accounts. And when I break bread with y'all, y'all get cash so if anyone wants to look at any of you, they won't see nothin' outta the ordinary. Those phones were how much?"

"Twelve hundred altogether, two hundred a piece," Heather stated. "We each paid four hundred."

"Those will go at six each so that'll be six hundred times which is $3600," Joker expounded. "Y'all gonna keep whatever come from the phones. That $5000 is y'all's to split right now."

"Fareal?" Imani's face lit up. She looked out the windows down the hallway. It was still chill out there and the officer was seated. "I… but after $3600 there's $1400 left."

"Watch the main door, Imani," Joker told her and grabbed Silas' computer. He accessed the Capital One Banking Site and showed the women an account he held there in his deceased father's name. "This account was in my dead Pops' name but I'm second on it. How much is in there?"

"Is that $103,000?! Okay, okay," Vanilla stated, moving over so all three of the nurses could see. And it had Joker's and his dad's names along with the balance inside of the savings and checking account.

"Wow. That's cool."

"I never…you are so mysterious," Imani told him. "I knew you were a baller."

He smacked his teeth. "That shitta barely covers the cost of my Mercedes or Bentley GT. That's cover money to keep the IRS off me."

His nonchalant way of waving off $103k like it wasn't nothing made him look cool as hell in the eyes of the small but very close crew of nurses who were not nurses at all. At least they were not "RNs." They were LPNs which were Licensed Practitioner Nurses. Joker knew that they had no doctor's powers but didn't care. In hospitals, an RN (Registered Nurse) could be making $40k-$50k yearly to start but many push even closer to $100k with all of the extra COVID-19 era overtime hours. In many prison systems, they rarely used bonafide men/women who attended a true nursing school via a 4-year college program. James T. Vaughn Correctional system "nurses" were only required the bare minimum like an 8 or 10 -week online certificate program they charged $1500 on their Visa Credit Card.

These *"correctional nurses,"* mostly poor blacks who can't afford Princeton University, Syracuse University, and such, find opportunities for employment in corrections departments because they could barely pass GED classes. Additionally, the quality of education was subpar but at the end of the day, nobody gave a fuck about the lives they'd been charged with caring for. Joker understood fully the cold ruthless thinking that went behind how the American penal system conducts medical care of prisoners. He loved the fact that Heather, Imani, and Anjanette Vida Silas (her real first, middle, and last name) were "scrappers" so to speak. They weren't "registered nurses" and he didn't hear any of them talk about furthering their education, in a way to put them in a better position. They weren't *completely* lazy but he could tell that they were the type that fantasized about a man who'd snatch them off of their feet and spoiled them with wild sex, shopping sprees, million-dollar foreign vehicles, and fancy travel all over the world in a private jet and a yacht. All the shit they see T.I. doing for his folks, Jay-Z and Beyoncé, Swizz Beatz and Alicia, Ciara and Russell, and others.

"Close the door," Joker told Heather which she did right away. "I'm sure y'all prolly Googled me by now. I'm lying?"

He saw them shake their heads. He gently pulled the lovely young Imani flush up against him and French kissed her. Lightly suckling her warm sweet tongue. She pushed her marvelous pretty titties into his hard-muscled torso. Her hands squeezed his ass and she felt her cunt awaken inside of her white satin panties. He put her right hand down inside of his pants, knowing that she was the only one who hadn't had him yet. Her mouth was watering like Pavlov's dog at the sound of a bell which signified that food was nearby. It was a human wonder how the body had defense mechanisms such as fight or flight reflex. It also had skin that sweated which acted as the body's air-conditioner when it got hot. But it also had pleasure mechanisms like inside of the genitalia of a woman. Bartholin's Fluid lubricated her vaginal canal when she got turned on to help make sexual penetration easier for her and her man (or her own fingers/dildo). However, these same fluids could also be seen as a defense because they also push harmful bacteria out of the vagina. Women only think of what they see inside of their panties as "discharge" but each day, that same discharge is saving her life from any number of viral and bacterial dangers.

As Imani felt his heart beating against her own she drooled because her mouth watered so much. Another pleasure mechanism. He sat on top of the desk after she pulled his pants down. "I asked about the Google y'all prolly did cuz y'all know 'bout the missin' $250k they allege we took from the bank," he said while Imani started trying to make his giant pole disappear into her beautiful Egyptian-cinnamon brown face.

"Your lawyer denies you or your team ever even stepped into that bank," Heather recalled, watching her girlfriend.

"I got the money stashed where water, fire, mice, or anything can't get to it," he moaned as Imani held his balls and the base of his slick wet club and it started going deeper and deeper into her throat. She face fucked. "Holy fuuuckkk, Mani baby!" he cried, watching her go.

Vanilla sat in the chair handling a phone call, her cunt soaked. She hung up the phone as Heather looked around outside. Joker pulled his dick away and French kissed Imani with both of his hands on her booty cheeks. It was a must he eat her ass. Mando. Out of all the JTVCC niggas who have been on Imani Henry's little ass it wasn't small at all. Regina Hall. Joy Bryant, the babe from *Get Rich Or Die Tryin'* with 50 Cent. The two females didn't look alike but their bodies/asses were just alike.

Joker didn't play with Imani. "Lay 'cross that desk and pull them buns open!"

"Oh my God…" she said, laying down as ordered. "You gon' do that? You like eatin' girls' asses?"

He didn't answer her because his face was already there. She cared to trim but not shave. The black hair around her pussy was a very dark glistening black. He smelled the musky female aroma which was an instant turn-on. She reached back and pulled her asscheeks open and she looked adorable and sexy doing it.

He rubbed his nose all around the outer and inner pinkness, then pushed it into her tiny asterisk-sized orifice. "You smell like coral… mmm… taste like the ocean's salty-sweet water."

He only ate that hot little asshole and juicy slit for a minute or two. "All y'all pussy so different! Y'all got a nigga thinkin' of a four-way polyamorous relationship."

They all heard it and giggled as he picked the small woman up. She reached down and guided the large bulbous head to the wet opening of her tight juicy pussy. She bit and moaned into the left side of his neck. As sexy as they looked fucking Heather knew she had to keep her eyes peeled so she went out to the triage desk where she called Vanilla who answered right away.

"Stay on. It's me at triage where I can see everything," Heather told her.

In the office Vanilla had her legs spread wide with her right pointer and ring finger slipping and slopping in and out of her bald Polynesian-British cunt while sitting in her cushioned seat.

"C'mon. C'mere, you bad lil bitch." He laid her down on the throw rug with carpet underneath. He was on top of her immediately, looking down into her beautiful light brown eyes. "You got a phat *pretty* fuckin' pussy. No babies yet. I can tell from that puffy flesh around da lips…"

He put the weight down and took all the air out of Imani when he pushed his entire monstrous length and width into her pussy. He grabbed her ass with one hand and skewered her little hot pussy. She growled in his ear and licked him there.

"Damn I wish you was naked!" he said.

"Fuck my sweet pussy, Joker!" she continued to grow into his ear. "Oooouuu, I love it. I can feel all my pussy honey on you. Drippin' on your balls. I want your cum in me."

Imani loved having his long thick shaft buried inside of her and having him pummel her with short, hard strokes. When she repeatedly felt his egg-sized cockhead banging her uterus wall and hitting her g-spot, she lost it right there inside of the office, where her orgasm yielded a copious amount of her cream.

"Ohh shit… cum in my pussy…" she begged as she threw her hairy little peach at him. "I want to feel your hot cum shooting inside of my tight little hole. Oh, cum. You're so hard, Daddy. Oh-"

He grunted, and stirred his ass and hips, causing his enormously fat dark beige cucumber to widen and stretch her inner cunt walls. In. Out. Slower. Then faster. Cockhead busted and expanded inside of her at the tip, controlling her pleasure, extending the wild rivers of her frothy cum. She was waking him to lose control, and he wanted more of her hot tight pungent pussy. He tried not to but he was hammering her bad little ass. He French kissed her, possessing her sweet soft lips. She had those lovely pillowy lips, not the skinny rubber band or pink bologna lips. He sloppy wet kissed her…

Fucking her deep. Stroking so when he bussed he would drown her insides. "Feel my balls over your anus, dontchu?"

Slap! Slap! Slap! The sounds went.

"Keep them fuckin' knees all the way back," he commanded. "Can't believe dis lil cunt takin' all dis cock in that tiny hole, Mommie! Imma cum all in you…you want my nut in there?"

Imani was popping that thing up, engulfing his long thick girth. Goosebumps were all over her. He was up on his forearms looking at her sweet face, wet lips, her scrub shirt pulled up, bearing her phat titties. "I *need* it. I need that nut, Daddy. It's been so long! Buss that nut. Cum in me. I want your cum in my pussy…Matter fa - - ohh my fuck! Oh God, Daddy. Spit in my mouth for me."

He did it. A regular request. Especially from these young freak bitches. He spit dead in her mouth, into her throat where it hit the tonsils, and she emitted a low sexy whimper. The way she looked at him made him come undone. He had perfect cock control for the most part. Joker Red was well-known in the Five Boroughs – and wherever else he went – for dick control and for having a penis the size of old school pornstar *John Holmes* or *Ron Jeremy*.

His balls got firmer and firmer, pulled up tight. He stayed planted deeply inside of the James T. Vaughn Correctional Center's nurse. They were now hugging one another tightly. Wrapped around each other like a mating couple of big Burmese Pythons. Imani was making sure she got banged good by that gigantic juicy love club. As he bussed his warm hot nut all up inside of her she was being tongue kissed by him. She actually screamed into his mouth.

"Oooouuu my gosh, look," Vanilla whispered as he slowly removed his monster penis from Imani's small, ravaged vagina.

It looked like a million frothy but clear bubbles that covered her hairy gash. Heather returned and joined Vanilla in licking Joker Red's dick clean. But as it pulsed with new energy they backed off.

"We are so bad," Heather stated, her voice low as Joker excused himself. He had to sweep, mop, empty the trash, clean staff bathrooms, and see if any other chores needed his attention.

They all had their jobs to do and Joker didn't want to get in their way.

"Hey, Hodges!" the OIC, or Officer In Charge, called out to Joker who was hanging out inside of the breakroom. Joker came to the officer. "Yes, sir, sergeant?"

There was a maintenance lieutenant and another regular officer standing there. Sergeant Jenkins was the laid-back OIC who ran Joker's area. "Yeah. Hodges, the paint guys are supposed to come up here for spot work and what not and I'd rather not have to watch three other men. If you can handle the painting I'll have them leave you supplies."

"So I'll be doing' you a favor you mean," Joker stated more than he inquired, in a joking way.

"Don't press your luck with the slick New York shit," Jenkins shot back.

"I don't want them up here either," Joker chuckled with his crazy job supervisor. Jenkins was cool as fuck and never breathed down Joker's neck even though he knew Joker was a known gang leader. He had a lot of power and respect in the prison. "They came up here to install that new sink, hit a pipe, and flooded half the whole place."

"Those were plumbers," Jenkins reminded him.

"Don't matter. A mess is made I get chewed out of it ain't done right," Joker pointed out. "Any painting need done I'll do it long as I ain't rushed."

The paint crew delivered all of the paint and supplies, and Joker secured them in an unoccupied room near the nurse's station. Joker smiled when he realized that the room was spacious enough to fuck his nurses in. There was a carpeted office area in the back with a small yellow sofa, desk, and chairs. Joker filled up a couple of buckets with steamy hot water, towels, a broom, and a mop which he used to clean it with.

Behind a large shelf was a floor-to-ceiling-sized piece of plywood. The way he situated the floor buffer, desk, chairs, and all of the paint/equipment, including a tarp and plastic sheeting, it obstructed the "bedspace" love nest. He laughed afterwards.

"What's so funny, sexy?" Silas just so happened to be coming back in from "Medication Call." She saw how sweaty and dirty he was. "Gosh… whattawe doin' here?"

"Real quick, walk alongside the wall, move da tarp," he pointed while directing. "Da tarp…"

"Oh, I can go…through here?" she was saying as she walked along the wall. "Oh, my! It's a space back here!"

She hurriedly came back out. "Wow…this is on our keyring, isn't it?" she asked.

He nodded. She had to leave, and he watched that ass swing as she did. *Jesus Christ*, he thought shaking his head.

CHAPTER 20

Dream, Dream, Dream

JOKER, Jamel, Holland, Rowan, Ruffin, and Blue Boy were all chilling inside of Joker's cell *choppin' it up, eatin' the fat,* counting it out the current cash take. Jamel AKA "Brook" had the *Suboxone Strip* coming in which they sold wholesale for $100 each. They took cash, Cash App, or Apple Pay.

Joker's brother, Al, hooked up with Heather and brought her crossword puzzle books that were manufactured by the Yakuzas and were laced with A-1 K-2. These Yakuza cats were professionals. The crossword puzzle books were nothing to bring in. No taste, no smell, and no spots were on any of the pages.

"Niggas," Joker said to his boyz. "There's fifty pages in these books. Long as I'm gettin' $750 a page we'll keep it comin' in. Each book to me is $37,500 and I ain't waiting forever, homie."

"Fuck you mean, J.R.? We got a time limit?" Brook asked.

"Buss it," Joker started. "So it's clear. We here in Tel-A-Ware to get these nigga's cash. Meaning, Imma give or…supply y'all wit one book. Don't bother with cuttin' the pages down to sell stamp-sized pieces for $50."

"That's how they doin' here," Rome informed Joker.

Joker dismissed the thought. "These niggas don't know how to stack bread. They just know *waste*. Check it. Take the inmate ID card…"

He took his ID card and used it as a pattern or "cookie cutter" to trace out "ID cards" from the first page of the crossword puzzle book.

"Ten full ID cards per page," Joker counted out bud. "$300 each card or $250 – up to you. Word of advice: Let that shit go at $250 because my plug is flooded wit it. So as fast as these are moved out the front door I got more coming in the back. So…"

"We got da picture, dog," Blue Boy stated, looking at the others. "Brook and Rome, let's do it where nobody steppin' on nobody feet. Y'all basically lead the Damus and I got the Crips. The priority gotta be for us to cover dat thirty seven-five (e.g., the $37,500 for the crossword puzzle books). That's nothin' when it's $250 per ID card."

"Agreed," Brook conceded and added. "Yeah, Joker lookin' out. Ten ID cards a page is twenty-five hunnid and multiply that by fifty pages a book is a hundred twenty-five tho. *Then* subtract the $37,500 that goes to Joker and his connect-."

"And mule," Joker injected that point into the equation. He also handed Brook a small calculator.

"Right. Mule." Joker did the math problem before he forgot it. "Take thirty-seven thousand five hunnid dolla bills from the one twenty-five tho…equals $88k."

They all smiled except Rome. "The only reason I ain't smilin' and jumpin' up and down happy is cuz if it ain't one bad thing it's another. And we in *Snitch-A-Ware*."

"Well, believe it or not, mufucka," Joker said, shrugging. "We got dat *King Kong K-2* – wit da fentanyl, heroin, molly, and meth laced in it, duke. On da streets we move it in potpourri. It's King on da streets, so why it ain't King here?"

Rome nodded. "Damn. So we basically splittin' nearly ninety grand for me. Blue and Brook and thirty-seven and a half goin' yo way. Aight… let's go do it."

Their meeting was over.

*Dreams of Cute Slutty Pussy

IMANI, Heather, and their friend, Vanilla Silas, all decided to have a girls' weekend starting on Friday, which was "payday" for the medical personnel. After having dinner at Panera Bread they all returned to the hotel they'd rented rooms in for Friday and Saturday. It was one large suite with two beautiful bedrooms inside of it that Joker's "extras" helped them pay for. What Joker didn't help pay for was the several sexy male strippers invited over to party with them.

Heather had conjured up the nerve to leave her husband because she was convinced that she'd be with Joker, Vanilla, and Imani. Her torrid sexual trysts with Joker and the girls had given her real and true tangible courage. Right now she was laughing and holding her hand over her mouth.

"I can't believe you guys didn't tell me!" HBS squealed as Megan Thee Stallion's club hit *Wet Ass Pussy* began followed by every other song where female rappers were talking about all the dick they could suck, pussy they could lick, and twerking they could do. The male strippers were some nasty motherfuckers, too. Very muscular, clean, very smooth, and hairless – (the nicely clean-shaven-kind-of-hairless). Out of the six men, one of them was Latino and one White. Heather was chosen by them and she couldn't believe that they were all over her, dancing for her while wearing nearly nothing as she heard City Girls banging in the background. "I know you heard me, Vanilla," Heather murmured.

The other four strippers were Black men. One was light-skinned with a ponytail. He and another male stripper were all over Vanilla as they sat close to the left side on the far end of the living room sofa.

"Girl, this yo pre-divorce party!" Vanilla announced in reply as she looked up into the eyes of the Colin Kaepernick looking dancer, who was all up between her legs, kissing on the blue jean-covered crotch between her thighs.

Vanilla was melting beneath his touch. She could feel a warm stickiness spreading down there, also. Her cunt got horny and wet rather quickly. She stared at the stripper and could tell that he had a great-sized bone. Her mouth watered instantly. She knew right then that it was about to go down because that's what these women did for Heather. They didn't hate her husband but they didn't like him that much either because he was very selfish. The *wham bam thank you ma'am* type.

"The name's Bumbo… Mami, what's yours? Mr. "Kaepernick" inquired of the Polynesian honey.

"Vanilla," she gasped as she lifted her ass up while he took her jeans off along with her wet satin panties. He slipped off the silk and velvet sleeve that covered up his manhood.

"Open wider, baby," he commanded sexily. Kissing her soft pink lips. "I need your knees up…your pussy cream drippin' into da crack over this pretty pink little asshole of yours." Her juices leaked like rain on a window into her tiny booty hole, too.

Without a further word, he started in on eating her wet creamy center, breathing in her earthy feminine scent. His tongue slithered west and east over her soft asshole, the skin of her buttcheeks below, and her tasty perineum. His nose nudged its way up into the furrows of the labia minora, the pulpy lips of the labia, and the dominant protruding clitoris. Every time his tongue flipped the top right side of her clit she was ready to explode in orgasm. Bumbo knew his way around the curves, cracks, and crevices of a female. Especially a really sexy one like Vanilla.

"You have soft pussy walls," Bumbo told her after he speared her cunt hole with his long thick tongue.

"I do?" she softly asked as she watched Heather deep-throating the stocky Puerto Rican man on a separate sofa. Behind her, the white guy was about to fuck Heather with his six-inch but very wide. Dude looked like a 20-ounce Coke bottle.

"You do. I shove my tongue all the way in a pussy and some are almost like rubber walls and some, like you…" Bumbo had a sexy smile with dimples. "I wish my tongue could fit in your asshole. It fits the tip and your asshole is soft and real clean."

Vanilla giggled and stretched her neck to stare over at Imani as she swooped & bobbed her sexy face-up and down over one of the other black male stripper's dicks. She likely wasn't counting sucks but she took one huge 8 ½ inch porno penis down into her throat about twenty times before switching to the other 9 ½ or 10 inch brown cucumber about as many times. While deep-throating one of them big, sweet, juicy dicks she jacked off the other. Imani wasn't joking. The first one could barely last seven minutes. She let him bust all in her mouth but it leaked back out on her hand down naked breasts. Then she finished off the other one. He grunted, and busted on her face and breasts.

"I only know *clean*, Bumbo," Vanilla toyed with him as Imani went to shower. "What's *real* clean?"

He smiled as she threw a 3-pack of condoms over at HBS. Heather nodded and took her men back to the bedrooms.

"You. Your anus smells like lemon shampoo or body wash," Bumbo tried to guess.

She smiled. "Good nose. Let's watch Heather get her pussy stretched out."

There were two rooms back there to the left and right of one hallway in the very nice hotel suite.

The dark chocolate, 5 feet 5 inches, 150 pound Heather was taking it like a *PornHub* Pro-T.H.OT. She was way past the tongue phase; she wanted to be stretched more than Vanessa Simmons in that *SonoBello* commercial where they advertise getting all that extra skin and fat cut off. But the only stretching Heather wanted was her pussy, her asshole, and her mouth, and just what the strippers were there for.

"Put them legs back!" the black stripper named Polo hissed, his sweat dropping all over her titties and her face. He had that gigantic dick, too, 9 ½ inches with a head on it almost like a doorknob. "Damn, you got a dark sweet lil pussy girl! Throw that shit at Polo, baby!"

Heather bumped into him. He was stretching her hot little pussy crazy wide.

"Somebody get my ass. I need my ass banged too!" Heather whined.

Polo rolled to his back. His dick plopped out but it was thrust right back in.

"Imma get in and out just like a robbery in that asscrack, baby. I love fuckin' bitches in they phat, tight asses," Bunk told her in his deep sexy voice. "Both of us already bussed in your friend's sweet mouth so you 'bout to get a long hard ride!"

The dick inside of her stroked slowly up and down while Polo shoved her breasts together. He already had her nipples in his mouth nibbling on them. Kissing each breast like he was worshipping her. She whimpered and shivered, shoving her gorgeous jugs more forcefully into his face, begging him boisterously, "Harder. Bite them. Bite my nipples!"

Bunk used a tube of tropical-scented AstroGlide sex lube which he applied by sensually stroking onto his hard throbbing man piece. The way Polo had her ass bouncing and jiggling as she slipped and slid on his stiff pole was a very sexy sight which had Bunk's dick hard enough to hit a home run.

"My dick feels like ten pounds of lead," Bunk said loud enough for Polo and Heather Beatrice Sampson to hear. "Ayo, Polo, you think she can handle both of us?"

"She handlin' this big dick," Polo answered, kissing her full lips. She French kissed him for nearly a minute while he reached down and lightly pinched her swollen clitoris.

"I never had a dick in my ass," she declared as she laid down on top of Polo. "But I fuck myself with my thumb while frigging my clit and I cum very hard when I do that. Plus I have a butt-plug vibrator that I put in when I masturbate and read sexy black urban street fiction."

"You mean books?" Polo was still fucking his huge bone in and out of her, hoping that he could last longer because Heather had some really good pussy.

"Uh-huh." She nodded, slowly taking that hard meat in…her fabulous ass ground down into him which smashed her wet quivering clitoris into his pelvic bone. Bunk greased up her asshole, with the AstroGlide lubricant, and she let out a long, drawn-out, cat wail. "Aauuunnnnh, it feels so wet and good how your long finger pushing inside my ass!"

Bunk added another finger and butt-fucked her tight anus while she made close-to-orgasm sex noises and pushed her pussy and asshole back onto the big dick and fingers inside of her.

"She ready to take it, P," Bunk told Polo as he spanked Heather's moist, sweaty buttcheeks. Bunk was a tall, brown-skinned man who had a bald head, a long beard, hundreds of tattoos all over, and light brown eyes. He was in fifty "when flavor" adult XXX-rated movies and counting. Bunk was *The Neighborhood Fuck-U-Man* for real. He got up behind her. She was already in the doggy-style position on top of Polo. He spread her knees further apart.

"Hey, Mama, how boutchu lemme see them pretty lil hands reach behind you…?" Bunk said in that deep sexy voice of his while leaning forward over her small back and licking her ear and the micro pellets of perspiration off of her neck. "Reach back here, spread them cute buttcheeks open."

"Uh-huh." She nodded because Polo kept tonguing her down all crazy and pushing his rock-hard dick so deeply inside of her. "You can't be kissin' me like that and ain't no ring on it."

Polo smiled and froze, trying his best to keep himself from bussing off inside of her. Sounds of women and men fucking, grunting, moaning, and sucking were heard throughout the room now. Vanilla and Imani were being fucked like rag dolls while swallowing loads of semen at the same time.

"Look, Imani, Heather 'bout to be double fucked wit that giant dick in her tiny bootyhole!" Vanilla panted from where she was on a nearby sofa.

The other women watched as the four other male strippers used the bathroom to shower and clean themselves up.

"Like this?" Heather was holding her lovely phat booty buns apart while her face lay to the right on his chest which was soaking wet with sex sweat. She lay against him, still impaled on his pulsing hot manhood.

"Hell yeah, baby, pull dat bitch all da way open…umm… you look all wet and creamy in there already," Bunk almost whispered. She had a lot of pussy juices and Polo's precum mixed in with the AstroGlide and Bunk loved the chocolaty brown ring around her tiny anus. "Your pussy perfume got this whole room lit up, baby. You got a wonderful scent to dat thing. I wish I was you man eatin' this pussy. I'd have this sweet ass sittin' on my face every day!"

She loved hearing that hot shit. Bunk spanked her and ordered her. "Push this fat little ass back. You ain't got a man to fuck your horny little ass, huh? You need a mufucka to bang you out, dontchu?"

"She getting divorced but she gotta man," Vanilla blurted out.

Bunk watched her impale herself back onto his stiff hard monster. He removed it, re-greased it, and buried it all the way inside of her the second her sphincter muscle collapsed. "Aaaaaiiieeee, *Fuccckkk!* FUCK! Fuck my ass, Bunkyyyy! Do dat shit. Both of you!"

It was hard to tell whether she never had a real dick in her butt because she hit the ground running. Well, *fucking* would be the more appropriate term. She went buck wild. Polo and Bunk were out of rhythm for the first couple of minutes.

"Let her set the pace, Daddy-O," Bunk directed his homeboy, Polo. "This ain't our first bitch together."

Polo nodded and suddenly gripped her waist and back as his nut went off and bussed gob after thick sticky gob inside of her. Polo even skeeted a stream of his seed on the inside of her thighs. He got of the way and let Bumbo, who was fresh out the shower, take his place. It didn't take long at all for Bumbo to take her wet pussy and for Bunk to give her an awesome ass-fucking. The strong smell of fresh semen was in the air thanks to Polo.

Bunk and Bumbo were both fucking Heather in perfect motion. As one dick sawed inside of her climaxing pussy, the other was being pulled out of her horny chocolate anus. Bunk was a seasoned butt-fucker, too. With the hardware built for her as well. His big dick head was like a doorknob so when it pushed in it stimulated her colon which seemed to be connected to her clitoris, breasts, and brain. And it was in the brain where all the chemicals like endorphins lay dormant.

As she was double penetrated, she fingered her clit underneath and when she bussed off, she thought about her new man.

"Joker…oh, shit, fuck me in my pussy, Daddy!" she muttered. "Fuck my ass with that big dick."

Bunk fucked her ass deep and hard. He was relentless on her tight rosebud-like backside. The act itself looked brutal and violent with the way his gigantic, intimidating meat kept pounding in at the dilating hole of her anus and her widely stretched open vagina.

"Grind it, baby! Fuck them dicks harder before we beatchu!" Bumbo growled, spanking her shaking ass on both sides.

She actually wanted to be beaten. "Oh my God! Keep spankin' me and fuckin' me!" she whimpered, burning her knees as she rode between the tub of muscular men. "Pull my hair, damnit!" she demanded.

Bunk was in some kind of Porno King's zone or something as he yanked the pretty dark-skinned chick's hair back and held her head with both hands while turning up the way he fucked her full-power and full-tilt. She kept on about this "Joker." Telling him to, "Fuck me in my ass, Joker Red. Fuck me so good. Stretch my asshole wide open, Joker darling. Imma squirt hot female coochie cream all over your mega big Clydesdale dick."

They wondered about Joker. To them, they couldn't care less. Heather was an beautiful hot fuck. Bumbo watched Bunk and together, they sawed in and out of her. Both men buried their large penises in her until they could feel their nuts touching. No man in their group considered themselves gay but they did do some weird things for that cash. The "nut-touching" was probably the least weird thing.

"Don't cum, baby," Bunk gasped. "Dontchu fuckin' cum yet, okay? Let us see you squirt."

Bunk let loose and let his cum blast off inside of her bowels.

Bumbo blasted his nut off inside of her warm pussy. She had his toes curling because her soft pussy was so good.

"You are one good fuck, boy!" Bumbo told her. "Keep playin' witcha clit. Make it squirt for us."

She was already on fire. Imani got on one breast and Vanilla on the other. Both women helped her masturbate by lightly massaging Heather's chest, her nipples, and her lovely breasts. Imani let her left-hand slide across Heather's belly and into her sperm-leaking snatch. The scent of sex was strong on her, but she was on the cusp of cumming her head off as Imani finger banged her. Vanilla sucked on her titties and Heather went overdrive on frigging her clit 100mph.

"Uum! Aann! Aann! Aaaaiiee! Fu—! Oh, Fuck! I'm cummmmm-ming!" Heather's fingers sounded squishy and wet as they went crazy on her pussy lips leading up to this moment.

There was a shooting, arcing, geyser of her body's backed up girl cream. Real squirters emit out orgasmic cream stored up inside of the woman's Bartholin's Glands called Bartholin's Fluid. All woman can squirt or "gush" when or if their clitoris and G-spot are highly stimulated simultaneously. Right now, her G-spot, her clitoris, and many other spots were lit up inside of her, causing her hips to gyrate desperately in a rapid circular motion then she relaxed and screamed when the cream shot out of her. It was one of the sexiest sights in the world.

"Glad this a hotel room," Bumbo stated, grinning over at everyone else. He collapsed over onto his back. "That pussy lemonade you blasted out everywhere gon' stain!"

They all laughed at the humor.

The men left during the wee hours of the morning but not before Bunk asked, "Who the hell is Joker Red?"

Heather was wrapped up in a black beach towel. "He's a god. We're his goddesses!"

They were all also tipsy by this as well, feeling no pain at all. After the male strippers' departure, Imani, Vanilla Silas, and Heather Beatrice Sampson, all slept on a humongous queen-sized bed in the master bedroom of the hotel's "Princess Suite."

"Sweet *Mary Mother,* my asshole is stretched out so wide!"

Heather exclaimed. "But with all his cum runnin' outta me feels so delicious."

"Tell me about it," Imani said sleepily.

"Goodnight pretty babies," Vanilla murmured.

They were eventually asleep. The exhaustion of the evening had finally completely overwhelmed the three women.

CHAPTER 21

The Hottest XXX Dream
<u>Was About Kate Smith</u>

IN JOKER'S UNIT, inside the building he was housed at in James T. Vaughn Correctional Center, he was fast asleep in his cell when he heard the unique sound of his door being opened with a key. Normally, the officer in the "bubble" or the security console would push a button that would or could open the door, but this person was using the only other key available to make entry into his cell or "room."

Joker, who slept in his boxers, leaped from beneath the sheet and blanket ready to do battle because this was something out of the norm.

"Hodges, it's me," a woman's voice whispered as the door made a clicking noise. "Hey, where -?"

Joker grabbed her with his hand, covering her mouth, standing behind her. "Miss Smith?" he asked surprised.

She nodded. "Shhh, I can get fired taking a chance like this."

It was a pretty white girl, a brunette with brown eyes. "Holy shit," Joker stated, a little flabbergasted because Kate Smith had just come back from maternity leave. She had been a little on the thin-like-Olive-

Oil side but her baby girl had made her inflate in all the killer curvy areas that counted. She'd looked like a boy almost before her months' absence but now…"Goddamn, you look good!"

She nodded. "I know. So do you."

"How was the marriage and the birth?" Joker asked, caressing her lovely round face. She was one of those milky white women who married her high school boyfriend or the first man who told her *"I love you."*

Joker knew what she wanted as she told him, "No marriage. I had a healthy baby girl."

He removed his boxers. "What…he ain't suckin' on that hot clit the right way? Or is his bone not big enough to make love to his lady?"

Joker was already up on her left side, undoing her black belt. He put his right hand down the cleft of her asshole and his left hand over her soft wet brown hairs and her pulpy cuntlips. He used the body lube dripping from her vagina to glaze her anal and his fingers worked magic on the white C.O. as they stood leaning against the wall.

"Kiss me? Please kiss me?" she nearly begged him.

"How long we got?" Joker asked, looking at the glowing red digits on his alarm clock. He delivered upon her cute pink lips, feeling her wet sweet tongue twirling his lips and washing his mouth, his washing out hers. Their kiss was one of those kinds that were meant to say something as much as it was meant to do something. His dick almost blew up the way she kissed him, and her little wet pussy nearly burst into a fireball.

"'Til 6:00 AM if we give staff Lieutenant DeJesus four hundred dollars," she said, undressing and getting under the covers.

Joker reached under a nearby towel and put the cash inside of her tactical pants. His eye caught the glistening pink reflection of her wet slice of mango. *Jesus, she had a gorgeous pussy.* He laid on his back and they 69'd like they were hungry to have each other's sex in their mouths.

"Oh my God… I needed this big black man's dick!" She was gripping that giant yellow banana piece and going ham. Kate wasn't no joke with the deep throat. She gagged several times but that was all part of the fun for her. She loved how his gigantic brown egg-sized dickhead slid down into her gullet like one of the big pelican or stork birds that could swallow a large fish or something. Kate just loved having that big ole thing pushing deep down into her throat again and again and again.

Joker had only fondled her and put her hand down into his pants to *"show her a giant surprise."* They'd did plenty of flirting and he knew her pussy was wet for him because she'd let him eat it a little bit *"just to see what pregnant pussy tastes like."* He couldn't believe it but she'd done it.

"Don't make me cum," he pleaded, pulling his skinny wet bone away from her. Kate was kissing the wet drops of pre-cum that fell from his open tip and cascaded down to his dick base and enormous balls. "Damn, you vicious wit yo head game, baby."

She was also in love with sucking on balls. She almost took in his whole scrotum. Looking at Kate, it was hard to believe that her small, cute mouth had the physical ability to take in so much man meat. But that was all a part of what made her so amazing.

"C'mere. I'm tryna…" He spread open her milky white cheeks and from the light glow of his television, he could make out the lioness' big face on her left asscheek and the scary face and mane of the male lion on her right buttock.

Joker loved women. He was so much of a man's man – an Alpha Male- that he got off on something so minute as the tiny hands and feet of women. And even without perfume women smelled so different – *good* different. Color didn't matter. How tall, big, or small didn't matter either. Not when it came to that wonderful female scent. Smelling women was like smelling flowers. If he didn't *like* a woman, if she was vindictive and shiesty for some reason, she didn't smell too good.

Kate? He was all over this little snow bunny. She smelled like the new Rihanna Christmas fragrance. He spread open the lips of her wet, warm, and fuzzy pussy and planted his thick four-and-a-half-inch tongue inside of her warm pussy hole. It was like having his tongue taste one of those Mango Yuzu drinks from Panera Bread, and even though his nose was mashed up against her asshole she smelled like nothing.

"Oh!" she moaned and sucked him slowly in and out while also soft-stroking his mighty pole in both hands. "Ohhhmmygodddyess, mmmm, glrrrrbp! Mmmmnn, glirrrpbp!"

She also played a sensual "slip n slide" game up and down his face, fucking her soft female goodies from his nose, his mouth, to his chin. And on each grinding move into his lips he'd catch her clitoris in between his teeth and circle his tongue around it in a 360° "clit torna-do," which woke her up and made her almost scream.

"Your tongue and lips are amazing," she cried out as she rode his face. Her fucking ass was riding and rocking. He held her cheeks open. She may have had a little sparse hair around her pussy but she was hairless between her booty cheeks. As her ass and pussy moved faster and faster to and from, he noticed how pretty her pink pussy crease was. It was a thin little seam with all the musky sweet juices coming out of it.

He paid a lot of attention to her clit which was erect and stood out more and more from the flesh that surrounded it. Plus, her little anus was pink and he couldn't stop licking it and thinking about it.

"You got...um." He maneuvered her onto her back and took off the black socks she still wore. "Fuck."

She broke out into a smile. "What?"

"Your back hole looks all tiny, pink, and innocent," he said as he got into a comfortable missionary position.

At the sound of his words, her pussy quivered and her anus clenched up. "Oh, my God, you'd never fit that thing inside of my ass! I mean it'd serve my fiancé right to get my pussy and my asshole knocked loose by this big monster dick you have. Look at me."

Joker was sucking on her bottom lip and he was already sinking his large man-piece into her sticky wet silky-feeling heat. "Yeah, baby."

"I really need you to make love to me," she urged him. "My dumb ass fiancé called inmates monkeys, and I believe he question the paternity of our kid. He barely touched me. I had to masturbate so – ohh, mmm, hoooo shit, baby, gimme that big dick."

"Just put your legs back," he calmly urged her, placing his hands up underneath her. He pushed in and started by long-stroking her. "Fuck yo fiancé when you a badass c.o. bitch. He don't wanna love you? Joker Red loves you. I love you, baby…I love you. Damn, dis pussy *good*! White girls got some super good ass pussy."

He was growling nasty words into her left ear that had her popping that cat and twirling it back up the large thick stalk of his hot full-grown man dick.

"You love white pussy? Whatchu love about it, you King Kong dick motherfucker!" she stated hornily. "Why you like *my* pussy?"

"My ego is on tilt right now cuz one of the baddest white c.o. bitches snuck into my room to get fucked by my big twelve-inch porno dick," he whispered while sinking that bitch past her uterus. She felt his beast sliding past her belly button and scraping over her clit. On each inward dive his tremendous brown cucumber made inside of her body quaked and melted. Joker knew it. He could actually feel when his extra-large bull nuts came into contact with the sensitive skin of the perineum and the membrane-like star of her pink anus, there was a sexy massage there that made Kate want to sob with pleasure. "And God, you bitches can take a dick deep and you love pain. You love how my dick stretching and hurtin' that sweet white pussy, huhn? Ooouu, baby, put them knees far back. I don't want nuttin' in da way. Gimme dat shit."

He kissed her slowly and massaged her beautiful breasts. She was full of his dark beige bone but that didn't stop her from rocking her kitty cat firmly onto his huge Alpha Manhood. Kate sweated a lot but he found it sexy how rivulets of perspiration pooled between her titties and soft belly.

"You can see it?" she gasped in a sexy whisper while latching onto his muscular back.

He was digging deep off inside of them guts. She was staring down at their sensuous pairing. Where his sex was penetrating hers. Her labia was swollen two or three times the normal size.

"See what? Me fuckin' that lil thing?"

She nodded but added, "I mean do you like how much I cum. How…I mean how juicy and wet you make it? You like the way my pussy honey soaks your big brown cucumber and drips down your balls? You keep makin' me cum on you!"

He grabbed her asscheeks and ran his fingers over and across her back hole which she loved and made her want him to fuck her three.

"Cummin' some more! Shit, shit!" she bit his eat and he kissed her again. Kissed her long. Very long. Her heart beat fast.

"Damn, we ain't wearin' nothin'. We ain't -"

The love-making turned into fucking and the wet *smack! Slap! Slap! Smack*! It was the universal language of skin-on-skin moist sound of a man and woman fucking. "Damn Miss Kate…ohhhh, my God. Ohhhhh, shit."

That gigantic, hard, soaking wet, real man dick was pushing in. Out. In. Out. In. Out. And, he was grinding, twirling, and banging that gorgeous thing *deep* inside of the cute, brunette correction officer as if it was their weeding night.

"Cum inside me, baby. Cum in me!" She was gyrating her sweating hips and fucking him back with her sweet tight little thing. She was one hot bitch. That fiancé of hers had a horny good looking white chick who had just had his baby a few months back and her pussy felt like a virgin cheerleader.

"Imma cum in your hot slutty little hole…" he promised, ramming her harder.

"That's it. I'm your slut Joker Red Hodges," she hissed while spreading her legs wider. "Anytime you need to fuck me I'm your slut…any time you want your dick sucked and balls licked…Oooouuu, all that creamy sperm in your white slutty pussy."

She held him tightly and pulled him close to her. "Damn, I was told right."

"By who?" Joker inquired, pulling his dick out of her purring kitty cat. Her cunt felt so relaxed and serene.

She lay on her left side facing him after glancing at the digital clock on top of his desk. She sat her walkie-talkie close by in case she received a warning to get out by her lookout staff Lieutenant DeJesus. She smiled. "You have a clean towel to dry all this sweat off?"

He did it for her, pushing moist locks and bangs away from her pretty eyes, and drying her with a towel.

"Words out about you," Kate told him. "Before I went out on maternity, I was this close to sucking on that beautiful thing. But me and my fiancé were supposed to be getting close and havin' our baby. When I took him in my mouth it was you that I was sucking. I had wet dreams about you where I was so horny that I woke up finger-fuckin' myself, pushing my silk panties inside my pussy. Another time my husband caught me masturbating while thinking of suckin' your giant dick and your warm tasty balls. I was squeezin' my breasts, pinching my pink nipples, I was even watering at the mouth at the thought of tonguing out your ass and eating up all the cum inside your balls. Doesn't that sound so hot?"

"You're the reason I love white girls," he declared, pulling her towards him on the thick mattress that was sold inside of the prison commissary. The regular JTVCC-DOC mattress was only called a "mat" because them things were barely thick enough to give a little puppy any comfort.

"Imani, Heather, and Silas are friends," she revealed. "We all know each other since middle and high school. We sucked a lot of dick together back in the day."

Joker dug the shit out of her. He kissed her. "Is that a favor you gotta pay back to De Jesus?"

"Officers are suckin' and fuckin' each other every day," she stated with a shrug. "He wants to fuck me – so what? No man can please me after what you've given me."

Joker felt her stroking him until he was as hard as Italian marble. She sucked and slurped him into her mouth. The way she gently fondled his scrotum and the balls inside made him even harder. She was one awesome and wild penis licker and dick swallower because she was able to take so much of him inside of her. She gagged but she didn't choke as she pushed her mouth and throat down in an attempt to swallow more of him like a sword swallower.

"I can't fuckin' baleev the size, Red Hodges. Look here…" She held her forearm up to show him that he had between his legs was flat-out inhuman. "See? Fucking astonishing. No fuckin' way was this beautiful work of art inside of my little cute honey hole."

It disappeared into her pretty face slowly, her tongue spinning around the corona like a giraffe tongue. She was one of the best dick and ball suckers ever. He knew what to do with her as he kissed her again and lubed her asshole up with a sweet scented sex gel. She was pushing her silky vaginal cavern and her pretty ass back onto his fingers.

"You kiss me like I'm yours," she whimpered.

"So?"

"I wanna be yours but I get this itch outta nowhere to become…" She got on all fours while he guided his over-size monster into her widely spread back end. "Oooouuu… I need to become a slut. I must be fucked and I have to suck black dick. I love cu on my tits…oh, fuck yeah. Fuck my ass. Push it in deep, Daddy. You love it. Can you handle all that?"

Damn.

This horny babe did indeed have a sexy white ass and a great shape to her boomin' body. She was able to take his long black snake into her steamy anal passage and because it didn't seem to hurt her he was able to fuck her. She urged him to fuck her asshole like he would her pussy. So he eased his monster out to the very tip and then he slammed it back deep down into her intestine.

"You can still be mine and be a nasty slut baby, I don't care. I just demanded my bitches be loyal." He made her turn over onto her back and he slowly re-entered her now pleasantly swollen rear end. She stared at him because he made love to her. The way he kissed women let them know if they were cared about by him. It wasn't all about bussin' a nut with Kate Smith, and she could tell. No man kissed her so *possessively* as he did. Her lips were swollen from the way she'd sucked his huge dick. The lips he was kissing now while softly and deliberately making love to her.

"You hear me?" he inquired in a whisper.

She nodded, loving the fullness inside of her ass. "I hear you. God that feels nice…so nice."

"You one of my women. Be who you are. Fuck dat fiancé dude. Fuck who you want, Katie. Suck who you want. No need to marry into madness," he advised her while picking up legs further and kissing her pretty feet. First the left one then the right. "I'll be your daddy, Mommie. That what you need? Huhn?"

She threw her asshole onto that big impaling dick of his. Meanwhile, her right hand was over her pussy. He could feel the light feathery touches of her fingers feeling the connection of his massive penis buried so far inside of her ass. Her clit was blown up twice the size due to it being so turned on.

"I'm bout to cum in your ass!" he warned. He leaned to the left and sucked on her cute toes. He was still able to pound the dick to her real good.

Her middle fingers were flying over her clit and she was gasping for so much air that her lips were dry and crusty around the edges. But she was most certainly having a series of multiple orgasms. Chart-topping climaxes where he was smelling the musky juices of her pussy as her nectar poured out of her vacant depths.

"Katie! Shit," he blurted and bussed his balls. Mad cum burst out of his huge pipe and filled her up so much that it leaked out down through her moist crack to pool on the sheet below.

"Oh my fuckin' God… I feel that warm juice spreading all through my intestine and belly!" she cried out pleasurably as she careened through another explosion. "Oooooouuuuu shit…my goodness. So sticky wet and warm inside my guts and my ass. I love it. I love you."

"Damn baby…ooooouuuu, yeah, you feel dat nut bussin' huh? You feel it cummin' in your ass? You love me fuckin' you and fillin' you up with the cum from my balls?"

He went to kissing her again, with his deep, toe-curling, way of kissing her. After they were all done she got dressed but they still could not keep their hands off each other.

"The $400 is inside of your pocket," Joker said as she put her long brown hair up in a ponytail. "You know where I am. Let's protect one another, okay?"

"I had the best sexy of my life," she complimented Joker.

"Me, too." Joker kissed her and let her go. She was definitely worth the $400.

CHAPTER 22

**In A Coma She Said To Him
"You talk and my anus opens up."**

Imani Henry, Heather Beatrice, and Vanilla Silas returned from the daytime medication administration detail soaking wet. They'd all just returned from their small five-day vacation. Joker didn't show up for his work detail at his usual time because his sister, Catherine, came to on her way to Baltimore. Once his visit was done he saw the nurses come through the main office as he and his homie Blue Boy were painting.

"Hi, Mr. Hodges!" Vanilla greeted him. She badly wanted to kiss him.

"Look what the wind blew in," Joker stated in humorous reference to the three hot females. "How y'all been?"

"Fine," HBS told him. She glanced at Blue who nodded at her.

"Y'all don't know da homie Blue Boy," Joker said to the ladies. "He from my projects Fort Greene up Brooklyn."

"Oh, they approved your request for the paint plan up here?" Vanilla inquired.

"Somethin' like that," Joker said. The nurses had a supervisor meeting but before they did, Joker was waved into their office under the auspices of removing the trash. He was provided with a dozen cell phones with USB chargers and S.I.M. cards for each of them. He put them into the large trash bin sitting outside and concealed them with another plastic trash can liner.

"Y'all went out and had fun like I told you to?" Joker asked in a low voice.

The women were all shy and didn't want to talk about it. But Joker understood. "Man, I told y'all to buy male prostitutes and celebrate HBS's divorce decision. And that meant to get fucked and sucked like crazy."

"We did," Heather grinned.

"You take it in the ass?" Joker wanted to know. He walked up closer to her so he could grab her hand real quick as other medical staff walked by the office.

Vanilla and Imani exited.

"Yeah." She beamed up at him her eyes big and bashful. "But not like when you did it."

"What was the difference?" Joker asked.

She sat on the desktop. "Um…they were strangers and it was just pure and wild fucking. When you…I mean with you…when you talk that shit to me before you ever touch me, my anus opens up. It's a hot, wet throb inside my ass. Kinda like pussy lube glands are in there. Those guys had big and thick dicks but only half of what you got, Daddy."

"It 'opens up,' huh?" Joker clarified.

She nodded. "Hell yeah. When you fuck my ass you rip it open but soon as you take it out and push it inside my pussy, my clitoris and my body explode in multiple orgasms."

"Heather!" Vanilla called out to her from down the hall where their meeting was about to begin.

"I gotta go," she told Joker who kissed her and slid his hand down into the front of her pink hospital scrubs and rubbed it over the warm gooey shit in the center. "Ooouuu! Shhhssss – don't. I'm so wet, ain't I?"

He nodded. "Damn, I need to bone your hot little ass. Is it opening up for me right now?"

She nodded and sashayed away with her phat ass jiggling like a Slinky.

"Blue," Joker got his attention. They walked down the corridor to where the supply closet/paint supplies and clandestine bed space were.

"Ayo, you know Amy, the white nurse, with the phat ass?" Blue asked Joker.

"Yeah, she fuck with Sergeant Carter," Joker acknowledged. "Look, run these phones back to your group."

"No cash? Did they already pay?" Blue asked.

Joker nodded. "Is that a question? They had to pay. It was cash app. Just be easy on who getting one cuz they get caught, we don't want to get told on."

"My name and yo name ain't connected," Blue assured him and exited down the hall with the big trash bin.

"Her Soft Pink Cavern"

IT WAS 7:00 PM and a thunderstorm with lightning strikes made the prison security shut it down for the night. Joker had his eye on his boy Blue for one moment and then in another, he had disappeared. Joker and other workers were ordered to grab mops, mop buckets, and towels to dry up flooding water in the areas that they worked.

Joker saw Blue furtively pulling the nurse they were talking about into their secret supply closet and he smiled. '*Bout time the nigga got some pussy*, he thought as he grabbed a squeegee and used it to push flooding water off of the linoleum floor.

"What's up, Bush?" Joker asked the dorky white officer who sat at the desk up front. He only nodded back at Joker.

"How many of you guys usually up here, Hodges?" Bush questioned him.

"Just me," Joker told him. "I should be gettin' one down here to assist on flood patrol. If it stops or slows outside I'll likely stay til the 11 PM shift change. If not I'll stay in the infirmary all night. You can fall back, I don't need nothin'."

That's what the officer did.

Joker went to the supply closet and closed the door behind himself. Blue Boy and Amy were both naked with Amy stretched out flat on top of a dozen or so blankets. Blue was holding her creamy white buttocks so wide open that Joker could see the light brown curls that lay wet against the outer labia that protected her soft pink cavern inside. And her anal crinkle had a light beige-tannish circular halo surrounding it and the inner part of the hole itself looked like it was an angry red color due to the harsh way he was gripping her ass flesh and prying them open.

But she liked Blue Boy's aggression. The way he was just taking her ass and pussy from her made her wet and very turned on. She'd sucked her man's dick at the prison but he was a correction sergeant. She'd always dreamed of being fucked by an inmate and finally, it was about to happen.

Blue Boy felt her body stiffen when he softly suckled on her perineum. It was exactly what she liked. She was a 5 foot 3 inch blue-eyed snow bunny with a fantastic body, and grapefruit-sized breasts, and she loved sex. Her husband barely touched her anymore and she found herself daydreaming a lot. She was a submissive woman and Blue Boy could sense it.

"I love eating out the asses of beautiful white girls. I'm so glad you a clean bitch," Blue Boy whispered as he presented his huge manhood to her. "Gimme them cute lips. You suck dick good?"

"I love sucking a big juicy dick…but yours is so fuckin' big." She rubbed his thick hot length on both of her rosy, red cheeks and he could instantly tell that she was deeply smelling his warm masculine scent. He made her mouth water.

She grabbed him down knowing that she was feeling eager and hungry to have such a pretty penis inside of her. His precum was like the salt on a sweet snack and she wanted to keep eating it and tasting it.

She spit on his giant shaft and slicked it with her small hand and fingers.

"You watchin' J.R.?" Blue whispered. He couldn't see around the corner.

"I'm here," Joker told him.

"You wanna fuck us both?" Blue asked her as she went ham on sucking him into her throat.

"Fuck me, Blue," she told him, laying back and spreading open her beautiful legs and thighs. "I just have to be fucked. Just by you, honey. Just by…"

Joker was nude by this time and when she saw the foot-long weapon swinging left and right between his powerfully-built thighs she suddenly forgot how to breathe. Blue Boy pushed his big log through the tiny dripping vaginal orifice. He wasted no time in fucking in and back out, then he slammed himself back inside of her until his scrotum covered her juicy asscrack and anus.

"Imani!" Amy tried to exclaim but the hot pole banging into her horny young pussy felt too damn good. The nurse Imani was pulled into the private room where Joker laid her next to her friend.

"Might as well fuck these hot pretty bitches together," Joker said as he pulled Imani's purple scrubs off. He sucked her long nipples and moments later felt Amy's right-hand wrap around the base of his shaft and squeeze him gently. "You like that black dick, dontchu?"

She let go of him when Imani licked his entire length. He took off her panties and almost immediately the pungent aroma of her feminine arousal wafted into his face.

"That's what I'm talkin' 'bout! I love when a pussy smells like a pussy," he stated in an informative but lusty way. Imani opened her mouth wide and ingested the gigantic light-skinned foot long cucumber-sized man piece into her mouth, but he only let her have about twenty or thirty sucks before he took it away from her. "Them dudes fuck you, too, Mommie? Did they fuck your ass, too?"

She shook her head. "I mean I fucked two of them with condoms and I sucked their dicks."

"Did you swallow?" he inquired.

He was on top of her now pushing his massive pole deep inside of her. So deep that if she touched her belly button she'd feel the throbbing neck and head of his long, thick pole. She always tripped how she could take that thing that Joker had hanging between his legs. He was like that porn start Lexington Steele whose penis was purported to be something like 13 or 14 inches.

But a most factual assessment of David "Joker Red" Hodges was that he was more like eleven no more than twelve inches. His corona, or the helmet on top of his circumcised art piece, was the size of an Indian Plum or a chicken egg. Because he was a yellow black man the color below was darker-sort of like the color of a brown egg.

"If you don't want me to party wit da girls no more… I promise I won't if you keep fuckin' me and givin' me this big sexy pipe, baby," Imani whispered. She lifted her pussy, impaling her aromatic, juicy little hole onto the pistoning rod thrusting into her. "Oooouuu, keep fuckin' me, Daddy. Make me yours. I won't fuck nobody else. I won't suck no one's hot, hard, dick in my mouth anymore even though I love my face bein' fucked."

"Oh yeah? This'll just be my ass?" he breathed while burying all but two or three inches inside of her. "First things first open them legs wider and say it again? You'll be my freaky slutty whore. I wantchu to say it?"

She stared at him wide-eyed, saying, "I swear it…Imma be your freaky slutty whore."

"And no more suckin' other men or eatin' their semen," he told her, putting her on all fours.

"No more eatin' semen, Daddy," she said, trembling as he forced himself back into her pouty pussy lips. He stared at her winking anus. He gripped her cinnamon brown buns and ground his humongous pole inside of her.

"Kiss Amy and suck her titties. Kiss my man first," Joker ordered her.

Imani didn't hesitate. She tongue kissed the breath out of Amy while squeezing her flopping and flailing white titties. They were all sweating in the warm closet now. Joker was pushing his soaked penis deep inside of Imani's fiery pink depths and watching her and Blue Boy tongue fuck because Amy was ready to buss her girl juices all over Blue's pounding dick like rain.

But Blue pulled Imani to him because he felt his pipe turn into heavy steel. "Damn Joker, I've been wantin' to fuck her for a long ass time. Hey, Imani, I know my shit ain't as big as his but I'm almost thick like a soda can at least eight inches, nine inches."

"Be my whore, Imani. Give my homie that pussy and make sure you swallow or let him cum inside your guts."

Imani went right over to Blue and sucked his shiny white and red Latino bone. Then Blue let her ride it on top while he played with her asscheeks and finger fucked her backdoor.

"Everybody in the prison thinks about fuckin' you," Blue murmured as he bit her nipples and squeezed the perspiring orbs while she hopped, ground, winded her wide hips, and popped that young pussy to and fro.

In the meantime, Amy was staring down at the long, thick, and mean sinister appearance of Joker's approaching weapon. He wiped the sweat from his brow and watched her watching him. Her right hand was already down between her legs massaging the inch-long erect clitoris. Her pink nipples were like the color of wine and they were also stiff and standing up hard and erect.

"You look scared of it," Joker stated quietly, setting the head of his pipe right at the tiny entrance of her pink cunt.

"I'm not scared," she lied. "But it's so big. Will it fit?"

"Let's see." He pressed inside of her slimy secret and she bit her lip. He fucked those first few inches in and out of her insanely tight pussy. "Your husband…is Sgt. Carter?"

She nodded.

"I'm 'bout to fuck his sex life up cuz your pussy gonna fiend for this giant inchman dick for the rest of your life." He kissed her like he loved her and he told her exactly that as she let her body and soul open up to take his monster dick. "But you my wife right now, Amy. I been dreamin' 'bout this phat ass… I always knew you were teasin' us inmates by not wearing panties, huh? Tell me."

She nodded. "I do it on purpose. All the women do it."

He was banging that heavy lead dick to her now. He had her pussy bussed open.

"Why? To make us look at y'all phat ass and bare naked pussies?" he asked.

"No." She was throwing her tight pink wetness back up at the impaling club. "To make y'all ducks hard so we can tell which ones to choose when we wanna suck or fuck."

"I love you, baby, you a sweet little white thing," he told her as he suckled her throat and neck. He wasn't just banging her, he knew he was close. He was fucking in and out of her pussy like a madman and Blue was doing the same.

Joker was launching his dick up into Amy's vagina like an intercontinental ballistic missile and her cummy nectar was flying all over his balls and in between asscrack and flowing over her asshole like a pipe had broken. She was splashing and orgasming her pent up cream like it was her last. Joker thought she was one wet female.

And Joker filled her up full like a water balloon with his hot molten semen. A delicious all-over feeling that made her pretty little toes crack. She instantly knew that Joker was right on the money when he'd cautioned her that he'd destroy her husband's sex life because she was already feeling the twitch inside of her musky depths telling her she needed to be dominated and "slut fucked" by Joker once again.

Amy got dressed and Joker slipped out first. Seconds later, Amy and Imani sauntered away up the hall and into the bathroom inside of the Triage Office/Nurses Main Desk.

"Damn, Joker Mufuckin' Red!" Blue exclaimed on their way to the Worker's Maintenance Room.

"Told you, but don't expect free pussy from these bitches all the time," Joker informed him. "Be generous to women and they'll return the generosity."

"Even if you go broke?" Blue returned.

"Nigga please," Joker laughed cynically. "I don't care 'bout no green paper! Hoez can have that shit. It makes them happy. Secure. As long as you got *women* you own the world because of that buried treasure they have between their legs. I never worry about money as long as I got women on the team. They all got gold between they legs."

Blue got the picture.

CHAPTER 23

Coma: Toscha Hollingsworth's<u>"</u>
<u>Ass Creamy Pussy</u>

IMANI HENRY WAS the friend of Deputy Warden Hollingsworth. Because Joker had not been in Delaware long, he didn't know that there was a very long, sexy, and scandalous history at James T. Vaughn Correctional Center involving the 5 feet 6-inch light brown skinned bisexual Toscha Hollingsworth. She'd started as a regular officer in the D.O.C. posted at W.C.I. the Women's Correctional Institution. That was what Imani and Toscha were speaking about after a steamy sex romp. They lay nude, cuddled up together while their bare wet pussies rested underneath the silk sheets that covered them.

"His name's David Hodges," Imani was saying to the more powerful woman.

Toscha smiled. "Well, see. While I was sucking on your clit I could smell the faint scent of him comin' out of you and I thought I was trippin."

Imani kissed her lovely face. Toscha was in her 40s now but her body was as firm as ever. She was one of them badass green-eyed females with a small waist, flat tummy, hips, and the titties of a 13-year old but her ass made up for it along with them lips that reminded him of Meagan Good or SZA. So the training bra chest could be forgotten about with all her other top jewels.

"Are you mad?" Imani inquired.

"I mean, I'm not threatened," Hollingsworth stated.

"He's an inmate," Imani revealed.

"What!?" Toscha exclaimed. "You could be charged under the P.R.E.A. Act!"

"You mean like you and that Russian pop singer turned boyfriend-killer?" Imani reminded her.

Toscha paused and smacked her teeth.

Years ago, before Toscha was promoted to Deputy Warden, she'd been a lieutenant of W.C.I. That was when Merlina Pavlovavic – a pop platinum, Russian YouTube sensation with blond hair, and blue eyes one could almost see through, was written up by a male guard and brought to Hollingsworth's office for the disciplinary hearing.

"You're a beautiful girl," Toscha had told her when the door was closed, and they were alone in the windowless office.

Merlina was 5 feet 11 inches with skin like snow. "So are you, Lieutenant."

Merlina had mimicked the compliment, and though she had a thick Russian accent, Toscha had completely understood her.

Toscha couldn't understand how someone so uniquely beautiful with her oriental eyes, and her talent, could be a killer. "It says here that Officer Stroud asked you to put your bottoms on and you refused three times."

Merlina giggled in a very cute way and licked her lips out of habit. "Is that what he says? No. No way can it happen."

Toscha had found herself amused by the younger woman.

"He's mad I'm dressed," Merlina had explained. "He found me come from shower one day. I drop the towel and apply lotion. He stopped to watch and asked me a question of Mother Russia."

"Questions?" the deputy warden.

"So I see – while I put the lotion between thighs like this…"

Merlina had simulated rubbing motions in between her white thighs, "I can show so I prove innocence?"

Toscha had felt her nipples harden but she'd nodded. "Go 'head."

The tall Russian girl, 19 years old at the time, had taken off her DOC pants, and turned her back towards Toscha. "Then I reach back and apply lotion to these. And Stroud – he likes." She'd grabbed her panty clad buttocks and rubbed them in circular massage motions.

Before sanity could set in Toscha had gone down on her knees before the Russian teen and took off the white cotton panties. "Damn I shouldn't be doin' this," the lieutenant at the time proclaimed.

"In Russia, the women guard wouldn't say that," Merlina had whispered while her super long legs had opened wider.

Toscha had gently kissed the dripping pulsating pussy lips. "What do they say?"

"Nothing. They just want me so they fuck me," the sexy platinum haired woman whispered. "Stroud wanted to fuck me but I don't want a baby."

Toscha ate the beautiful pussy and finger fucked her first with one, then two and then three fingers telling her. "Nobody else will be fucking you. Only me."

It had ended that day with Toscha and Merlina's pussies grinding on the carpet floor of her office. Toscha had been almost obsessive over the young prisoner. Until word had gotten out to the Warden of W.C.I., a male named Shelton. He ended up with his penis down Toscha's throat before she had left W.C.I., only too late become Deputy Warden of JTVCC.

"I love him, baby," Imani told Toscha now. "I'm sorry for bringin' up Merlina. I just want you to know so -"

"So I can protect you?" Toscha asked defiantly. Imani frowned, "It ain't even like that."

"Ain't...like...ohhh, Imani, baby," the sensuous older sexy woman groaned when Imani kissed her way down Toscha's belly and buried her face into her warm soupy wet vagina.

Imani ate that woman's cunt out so good that Toscha thought she'd have a brain aneurism. Imani even fist fucked Toscha until she couldn't take anymore.

"Damn, baby," Toscha breathed hard later. "So what you're sayin' is what we have isn't over."

"Not by a long shot," Imani promised as their pussies kissed and did a jot sexual grind. Imani's asshole and pussy could be seen as it humped up and down over Toscha's. The overheard mirror showed the glistening wetness up and down the slice of Imani's brown asscrack.

She kissed her sweet boss and then strapped on a large black dildo. "This is how he'd gonna fuck you, baby."

"I don't fuck men," Toscha whispered as the dildo went inside of her. Her wide hips gyrated and rocked back and forth. "Not for ten years."

"This man's different." Imani pistoned in and out of her tightly gripping pussy with the big dildo. She plugged her cunt real good for at least twenty-five to thirty minutes. "His dick's like Lexington Steel's dick almost with balls like two juicy big plums. He has a long thick tongue and he's the most sexy ass eater alive."

Toscha's pussy skeeted and gushed at all the hot XXX-rated talk. Almost or similar to "SEX PUSSY" on IHEARTRADIO. Imani just talked of Joker like he was a god.

"Jesus!" Toscha gasped after they were done fucking.

The sheets were so wet that they had to pull up and lay on top of a blanket to stay warm and dry.

"A ass eater you say?" Toscha mentioned.

"That man he's just in love with you already and he ain't even met you." Imani assured her. "Please trust me. And he's so fuckin' nasty."

"Like make the skin crawl or sexy nasty?"

"Nasty like putting up a portrait of him in the living room suckin' our toes nasty," Imani replied. "I mean no shame. Looking at his foot long dick you'll be like I'm running. No way. But he makes a woman's pussy and anus open wide and next thing you got that whole gigantic porn king dick buried to the hilt in you."

"A foot. A real *foot*?" Toscha inquired.

Imani showed her a photo of Joker sinking that monster all the way inside of Vanilla's back-hole and again all the way inside of HBS's ass.

"He's fucked all of you?" Toscha noticed.

"One woman can't handle him. He's a bull. And I don't want my insides torn apart every day," she said. "Plus, he's Army Ranger. A hero over there and when he comes home…think of all that awesome dick we can all share…fuck…and suck."

Toscha was smiling. "You dick whipped…like that *KITE MAGA-ZINE* freaky book by *TANIA MARIE, SHE'S DICKMATIZED.*"

"The man's a winner," Imani told her. "And he smell mad good, too. No bologna balls and his ass ain't all hairy and funky. Trust me, you gon' have ya tongue all on his lollipop!"

By the time the ladies fell asleep Toscha was already dreaming about fucking and sucking Joker Red's big juicy pleasure stick.

CHAPTER 24

**Coma: "Inches of big dick
<u>down the Deputy Warden's throat."</u>**

THE MOST POWERFUL position inside of prison was "Warden" and right beneath the Warden was the Deputy Warden. Miss Hollingsworth held power at JTVCC and as luck would have it the actual warden was on leave for the next 30 days due to him being activated to military service.

"Hey, Gladys, what's inmate David Hodges' schedule for tomorrow?" Hollingsworth asked her assistant.

The petite white woman looked up Joker Red's prison schedule. "Infirmary worker seven days per week."

"I want him in my office for *clerical interview* position at 6:00 AM." Hollingsworth ordered. "You take the day off tomorrow."

"Thank you. I'll send the call slip to him," the middle-aged secretary reported.

Joker hadn't asked for a clerical position inside of the deputy warden's office. When he got the slip of paper he was curious. Everyone knew Toscha Hollingsworth. She was one of them really pretty 40-plus females every eye followed when she walked by. So, Joker showered extra early, put the lotion on with the Burberry cologne, and made sure he was all the way 100% fresh before going up to the Administration Offices.

"Hodges," Toscha called to him from her office as soon as he came in.

"Deputy Warden," he said, walking by her.

"I've been hearing a whole lot about you," she said, taking a seat in a large black cushioned chair.

He'd observed the curves on her body beforehand.

"Yeah I know," he stated back.

She smiled at his confidence. "You know? Well, since you know, what am I supposed to do about it?"

"Hm," he murmured. "I kinda got a feeling that a pretty young lady like you already got that part figured out."

She watched him walk over to where she was sitting and he stared down at her. "Feel my heart beat."

"I can see the jugular vein jumpin' in ya nec, Mama," he told her. He looked at the door. "Is it locked?"

She nodded.

"How long do we got, baby?" He was already undressing.

His shoes, socks, pants, shirt...he turned to face her a foot away where she could feel his body heat and how good he smelled. "Two, maybe three hours. B-but I can't...or won't take...have mercy you really are a goddamn horse. I can't do anything with..."

He picked her up and kissed her. She melted and put both of her warn hands onto his piece already hard. A jolt of electricity went through her, stopping inside of her clit. Her mouth watered for a taste of man. She whispered something about being with females for ten years and how nervous she was.

"Just grab that bitch and go for it, Toscha," he coaxed her once she was fully nude. "Just grab, kiss, and lick... don't you dare be sweet and shy. You da Deputy Warden livin' out a fantasy. Go 'head. Be slutty and nasty like I like. I hate careful, scary, and too cute bitches."

She did exactly what he said. She dove down onto the giant head of his yummy circumcised dick and spit on it. She used her long lesbian tongue to smear his saliva all around it. Rolling and pumping her fist up and down. He grabbed her hair and pushed several inches of the slick shiny shaft inside of her throat exactly how she loved lovers to grab her head. Her spit-filled grunts and moans were covered up by the oversized dick disappearing down into her throat. He laid back on the long black office sofa and watched her lay on her belly between his whispered thighs.

As she started to get into it, she could feel her pussy convulsing and he was smelling the aroma of hot cunt steaming up the air around them. Joker's nose never missed that coochie scent which was why he leaned forward and under to first grab her breasts. Her ass started humping up and down and twirling in teeny, little circles when he pinched her needy clit nubbin. The lips swell up with her increasing need soaking his hand. Her pussy was a wanton pocket of desperation, as well as her back hole which his left fingers found and massaged her warm vaginal cream into.

"You doin' good, Deputy Warden," he congratulated her and urged her. "Stick that pretty face against that shit, suck them balls."

She rubbed her face all over the super big sex weapon. Fucking her mouth harder and harder, almost wanting to make herself choke due to her need and desire to have and to be taken by a real man. "SHIT. FUCK. GOT-DAMN. Stop! Stop! Stop!" he gasped while pressing more of his girth and length in and out of her throat with her bubbly saliva sloshing all around, spilling and cascading over his thick staff and balls.

She whined when he snatched his enormous rod away from her and swung his hairy yellow legs over to the floor while she wiped her mouth with the back of her hand. He loved the curves of this woman. He stared at her spine and pretty shoulders. He reached out and gently grabbed her ass and he stared at the way her hips flared outward.

"Don't move, Deputy Warden," he whispered as he stared at the mesmerizing deep crack of her light brown buttocks. She still lay across the couch, both of her legs crossed, looking like urban/Instagram/sexy magazine model "Koko". "Don't move, Mami. Damn, you sexy. The way ya gap showin', small lil coochie hole look like a belly button."

He kissed both extremely soft asscheeks and pried them open. He buried first his nose inside the creamy treasure buried against Toscha's excited bare pussy. He sank two fingers inside of the fiery pink leaking hole and she was in a frenzy of squirming her ass back into his face. She smelled clean and delicious, fresh and forever wet. He was thinking, *Yeah, she got a mad clean pussy and her asshole smells like spring water. And I know – I just know she thinkin' of me buttmaning that little pucker.*

Her lips stiffened as he gently sucked her erect clit. It was erect like a small dick and going crazy. Her love juices continued to drip and flow as she pushed her fine ass all up and down his face. She was ass-fucking his nose with her little asshole, and it was making her more turned on and ready to cum. Her hands were no longer free. She was reaching back and pulling open those buns for her inmate Joker Red Hodges.

"Keep fuckin' my face, Toscha!" he gasped. "I love that lil pussy and your anus fuckin' my nose!"

She saw him get one knee firmly planted on the sofa and he was on top of her back and ass when he let the head of his majestic man-piece stake claim to that wet snatch. Four inches slipped in slimy but rubber-band tight. She was tight as tweezers. He knew she might as well be a virgin like 1980s Madonna *"touched for the very first time"* but one that was on fire.

"I need this forbidden dick!" she gasped and pumped it back and front, she was taking more. Five inches and he was Coke can fat, but her sugar walls were starving for a gallon of man semen. "Take it. Fuck this pussy please ooooohhh, god, uhhh… I need it hot and freaky."

Missionary style. She wanted to stare into his lovely green eyes.

"I told you don't be shy. Be slutty, Mommie. I love dirty. Nasty. Freaky. Forbidden. We can be as forbidden as you want," he whispered while lacking his arms under her armpits and clasping her shoulders. She put her legs back, and then he hit the button inside of that sticky wet thing. "There we go…deep. Deep. Forbidden. This what you like?"

She nodded, sweat pouring off her. "Please, Joker. Just keep it between us but I swore off men because my mother's brother took my virginity and her never stopped fuckin' me. We were Catholics. He even fucked me in the church. You like hearin' that? Your dick is getting' even harder as I fuck you and tell you this story."

"Hell yeah. It's forbidden and wild and sexy," he admitted as he fucked her even harder.

Her phat ass pussy had her juices frizzing and geysering out all around his impaling monster meat. The wetness and plain of proof of her sinful pleasure was frothing and bussing out around the sides of Joker's Mr. Porno King penis, it was all over the place. Soaking his belly, his dick and balls, every damn thing.

It was like they were inside of a sauna, the perspiration was flying off them. He switched positions and sat down saying to her, "I smell your sweet steamy body…"

"Huh?" She reached between her legs and stroked her entire hand on his huge tennis balls, jerked on his pussy juice-soaked dick, and then she masturbated the tremendous chicken egg-sized penis head on her erect clit for at least a full two minutes. "You a freak nigga just like Uncle Dino…my Uncle Dino."

He re-penetrated her but this time he made her sit her asshole down cowgirl style on him. She loved pain and was able to take it because he had "opened up" her ass for her. She moaned and grunted out lustful passion as she relaxed with her back flush against the left side of his body, her legs opened wide, her pretty feet planted on the sides of the sofa.

"Here…" she rubbed her soaking wet left hand all over his face, nose, and lips. "This what you want? You love that musky female sex smell, dontchu? I know you do. I love pushin' and fuckin' your handsome face with my ass… you make me feel so sexy, Joker."

She felt stretched to the extreme and knew her asshole was ripped but that pain made her more horny. Together, they masturbated her clit. He grabbed and squeezed her tits with the other. His full length was inside of her shitter and she was riding him hard. That pleasure mixed with the pain made her hotter and hotter and the cunt juice kept flowing over their hands and falling over his nuts.

"God damn, Joker!" her voice was a low hiss. "Tell you what, baby. You keep fuckin' me 'til I get pregnant…"

"You want a baby?" he asked while he picked up the pace. "Powerful woman like you – hell yeah, Mama! And what I get?"

"I know you been fuckin' dem nurses," she said as she backed up in a frenzy of extreme wanton lust on top of his long thick dick. "You get them, my protection, and I'll push to have your parole signed early."

He took his hard dick out of her. "You doin' it backwards."

"Why'd you-?!"

"Push for parole now and I'll fuck you like a madman every day!" he urged her. "You got the power to get me freed early then I'll move in with you."

She relented and got down on all fours with her face in a sofa pillow. He got back in that ass and gave her an award-winning porno fucking. It surprised him in the least that a tall, top-notch babe like her could handle him slamming all of that bone inside of her tight asshole.

"You don't know how bad I needed it. Harder!" she commanded him. The office smelled like sex and sounded like a pornography studio.

"Damn I'm 'bout to -!" he breathed against her ear as he laid flat on top from the back. "But not in your ass. In this pussy…

He worked his big brown cucumber up into her swollen vagina and she caught the rhythm fucking him back stroke for stroke. He fucked her pussy hard. Then suddenly both of them started to cum. Joker drove hard into her.

"Work that motherfucka, bitch," he ordered her as he pounded her. "Sure you want all this nut up inside that pussy? You want a baby, don'tchu?"

"Your baby."

"Shhhiiittt!! Arrrrgggggghhhh, cummin'!" he shouted and gobs of it spilled inside of her. "Take all that hot cum, Toscha. Slutty freak Toscha."

"Mmmm, ooooouuuu... I love the feel of it," she whined. "God yes, keep cummin' in my pussy!"

Joker was home in a matter of 90 days living inside of a house with all of his nurses, keeping his promise with Toscha Hollingsworth...

"He had a split in his tongue, he ate the beating hearts of rabbits that he caught and he sharpened his own teeth. He later picked up two young girls from a bar, took them to his house, where he killed them and ate them."

From Docu-series: The Devil You Know
about [Serial Killer] John "Pazuzu" Lawson

CHAPTER 25

Joker Awakens, Sinister Evil Smile
"Loyal To The Death"
West Palm Beach, FL

JOKER COULD HEAR his own heart beating as if it were sitting on a table next to him. He started breathing fast because the illusion was too real. *Am I high?* he asked himself. He thought of Imani, Vanilla, and the other nurses he'd been fucking inside the prison and…

It wasn't real. None of it. They would later tell him that he'd been wet dreaming-semen squirting everywhere. Uzenna and his other wives had to wrap his man up with baby diapers. They got a great bunch of laughs out of it.

He heard and saw a vision of Ghostman and that was the moment when he'd regained consciousness. In the private hospital, they'd transported him to in Jasper – where he had around-the-clock armed security – Iani, Uzenna, and Coral were in the room with him when he came to.

They screamed with excitement, the doctor and nurse came flying in to check his vital signs and gave him water and plenty of other fluids such as coconut milk, orange juice, and a liquid meal.

"We gotta get out," Coral told him. "They gonna kill us all."

"*What da fuck*, Daddy?" Uzenna asked, wiping her tears and lying next to him.

Meth Man Ace, who was the main chemist for the organization, came when he heard. He ran the industrial-sized meth labs not even a half mile away from the Jasper Estate they'd bought.

"Calm down, Coral," Joker stated as he ate mango slices. "Where we at?"

A dozen of his EIE soldiers entered. They hugged him. Bushwacker, strapped with an AR-15, only stepped into the room with tears pouring down his face. He locked eyes with Joker, they nodded at each other and that was all that Bush needed.

"Loyal to the death," Bush said.

"Loyal to the death," Joker stated.

"Them men love you," Joker revealed.

"WHAT!?" Boo snapped, which was everyone else's sentiment.

"Yeah." Joker explained. "Folk and EIE never clashed. But from outta thin air the GLP provokes me by this bastard pickin' up Natasha and fuckin' her? I mean she grown and do what she wants but these streets have translations average Joe motherfucker can't understand. And then Vinnie pops up in New York at the same time we in B-K to liberate Sis? That ain't flyin' wit me. It's too coincidental."

"So." Uzenna stated with a shrug. "Am I the retard factory? What am I missin'? How you equate all that with Steven 'Ghostman Dinero' Adams bein' alive? Did you see him?"

"He's dead, boss," Bushwacker said.

"He's Folk's *cousin*," Joker revealed. "Don't forget Jessika Cicero was Vinnie's mistress. And though we were cool wit da Bragas, it ain't no real love. Just millions of duckets that exchanged hands. They prolly want Meth Alley back. And if I'm murdered then y'all are weak."

Bible was thoughtful. "B-but *Ghostman*?"

Joker sat up. He was weak after seven days in a coma. He nodded. "That...I *saw* him. But I didn't see him. He's the reason I came back from the dead. From the comatose. When we did the execution he was able to bring the back seat down and pull it back up, shielding himself from the explosion."

"How do you know?" Uzenna probed.

"It's somethin' I would've done," Joker told the group. "I trained a lot of y'all. We had to step away from the blast because of the shrapnel."

It was a very believable theory.

"He used the emergency latch and got out the trunk," Boo visualized for all to hear. "And that cold in the Dakotas…any one of us could survive it with one eye closed. He built a fire and hid up in the Mountains 'til he could access his money I bet. Then he put his plan in motion. Aight." Boo paused. "Leah and your sister been runnin' everything. What's next?"

Joker smiled that sinister evil smile of his and said, "We gon' do what we always do. We gon' hunt down our enemies one by one like dogs. I want teams, mercenaries who are unattached to us, in Chicago and Brooklyn to annihilate the Bragas and Gold Lion Posse. And once they die – cuz they'll die – we'll go in and sweep up behind them. And we'll use Nina, Naomi, all our CIA and FBI contacts to flush out Ghostman…"

"Yeah, but how do you kill a Ghost?" Bible asked. "They tried that wit Jesus."

Joker stared at Bible. "How much you wanna bet we abouts ta find out?"

THE END

CONTACT THE AUTHOR

The Author: Lou Garden Price, Sr. can be contacted via email:
IGHOSTWRITEBOOKS523@gmail.com
100 Briar Drive
Rochester, NH 03867

Thank you for reading *HITTAZ 1-6*.

Did you enjoy the read?
Let us know how much by leaving us a review on Amazon and
Goodreads.

OTHER BOOKS BY

Urban Aint Dead

Tales 4rm Da Dale

The Hottest Summer Ever

Hittin' Licks For The Holidays: Atlanta

Wet Dreams On Lockdown: The Nurse

How To Publish A Book From Prison

By **Elijah R. Freeman**

Despite The Odds

By **Juhnell Morgan**

Good Girls Gone Rogue

Good Girls Gone Rogue 2

By **Manny Black**

Hittaz

Hittaz 2

Hittaz 3

Hittaz 4

Hittaz 5

Coldhearted

Coldhearted 2

Coldhearted 3

By **Lou Garden Price, Sr.**

Charge It To The Game

Charge It To The Game 2

A Summer To Remember With My Hitta

Snatched Up By A Hitta

Santa Sent Me A Real One For Christmas

Wet Dreams On Lockdown: The Unit Manager

Thug Me The Right Way 2

Thug Me The Right Way 3

Seizing A Gangsta's Heart For The Summer

Yours For The Taking

Wrapped Up In A Hitta's Love For Christmas

By **Nai**

A Set Up For Revenge

A Set Up For Revenge 2

Wet Dreams On Lockdown: The Librarian

By **Ashley Williams**

Trickin' On A Heaux For Christmas

Homie Hoppin' For The Holidays

Wet Dreams On Lockdown: The Female C.O

Letters Of His Love

By **Telia Teanna**

The State's Witness

The State's Witness 2

The State's Witness 3

This Time Won't You Save Me

This Time Won't You Save Me 2

His Summer Side Piece

A Holiday Heist

By **Kyiris Ashley**

Stuck In The Trenches

Stuck In The Trenches 2

By **Huff Tha Great**

Melted The Heart Of A Menace

Wet Dreams On Lockdown: Lieutenant Grace

By **P. Wise**

Merry Trapmas

By **Mia Sky**

Thug Me The Right Way

By **DiamondATL & Nai**

Wet Dreams On Lockdown: The Counselor

By **Paris Iman**

Wet Dreams On Lockdown: The Male C.O

By **Tamyra Griffin**

Wet Dreams On Lockdown: The Captain

By **TN Jones**

Wet Dreams On Lockdown: The Warden

By **Shawnice**

Atlantastan

Atlantastan 2

By **Chris Green**

IN The Streetz

IN The Streetz 2

IN The Streetz 3

IN The Streetz 4

By Tron Hill

Hittin' Licks For The Holidays: New York

By Freshh Moneyy

BOOKS BY

URBAN AINT DEAD's C.E.O

<u>Elijah R. Freeman</u>

Triggadale 1, 2 & 3

Tales 4rm Da Dale

The Hottest Summer Ever

Murda Was The Case 1, 2 & 3

Hittin' Licks For The Holidays: Atlanta

Wet Dreams On Lockdown: The Nurse

How To Publish A Book From Prison